"Are you firing me, Blye?"

"That rather depends on you, my dear Nicola," he said coldly.

For a long moment they stood looking at each other. *I'm crazy,* Nicola thought. *The battle lines have been drawn. Blye is my adversary. And all I can think of is how I long to be in his arms.*

She curled her nails into the palms of her hands. "I will not apologize."

"That's your final word?"

"Absolutely."

"I see." Blye smiled, a lazy smile that made Nicola infinitely uneasy. His eyes moved deliberately to lips that quivered despite her effort to control them, to her throat and then down to breasts he had caressed that morning. He was still smiling. "I see," he repeated. "Well, Nicola, you have only yourself to blame for the consequences."

ROSEMARY CARTER
is also the author of these

Harlequin Presents

and these
Harlequin Romances

Many of these books are available at your local bookseller.

For a free catalog listing all titles currently available,
send your name and address to:

HARLEQUIN READER SERVICE
1440 South Priest Drive, Tempe, AZ 85281
Canadian address: Stratford, Ontario N5A 6W2

ROSEMARY CARTER

lion's domain

Harlequin Books

TORONTO • NEW YORK • LONDON
AMSTERDAM • PARIS • SYDNEY • HAMBURG
STOCKHOLM • ATHENS • TOKYO • MILAN

Harlequin Presents first edition August 1983
ISBN 0-373-10615-7

Original hardcover edition published in 1983
by Mills & Boon Limited

CHAPTER ONE

'YOU'LL go in next, Miss Sloane.'

Nicola glanced at the receptionist. 'Next and last,' she murmured, adding silently to herself, 'and in this case most definitely least!' The tanned and wiry appearance of the other applicants had not escaped her notice. All had the look of athletic competence associated with a safari tour-guide. Smoothing down the skirt of her red and white sailor-style dress, Nicola finally allowed herself to admit to doubt.

Had she been foolish to give up her secretarial job—unexciting but not badly paid—to fly to Nelspruit for this interview? Foolish? Crazy was the word Maggie had used. 'Using your savings to chase a crazy dream,' she had scolded, though gently, for she'd known that Nicola's emotions were still too raw to stand much battering.

Yes, perhaps she had been foolish and crazy. Enraged by Jonathan's perfidy, as she thought of it, she had acted on what had probably been an irrational impulse. But now she was here, and the state of her finances as much as her pride made it difficult to go back. She had no option but to make the best of the situation.

Looking around her, she noted the bright animal posters, the antlers on one wall, a clay pot with bulrushes and dried proteas by the counter. Cheerful efficiency was the impression created in the reception office of Delayney Tours. Efficiency was the quality that would be wanted in a tour-guide. That, and experience.

Her heart sank a little at the thought of the last word. The ad had stressed experience. In her frenzy to get away from Morgan's Agricultural, from Jonathan and her typewriter, she had discounted her lack of experience. It had not seemed important. Now, in the offices of Delayney Tours, and having taken the measure of the applicants who had preceded her, she wondered why it had not.

She could, of course, walk out. Take the little money she had left and use her return ticket to fly back to Durban. Find a job in another typing-pool. Perhaps Morgan's would even take her back. . . .

No! She had not come this far to turn coward. Jonathan's perfidy had taught her one thing at least—no reason why she should not indulge in some of her own. 'Don't tell them you've never guided a tour in your life,' Maggie had advised when she'd realised that Nicola's mind was made up. 'If you've really set your heart on this job then lie through your teeth if need be to get it. Don't tell them you've no experience. You'll pick it up as you go along—you'll have no choice but to.'

Sage advice. Even now. She had every intention of following it. For she did want this job—very much. It was a combination of wanting to make a new life, of a long and natural affinity with animals and the outdoors, and of having spent a darned sight more money than she could sensibly afford in coming here. She wanted the job. She intended to have it. If that involved lying—stretching the truth sounded better somehow—then she would have to do it.

So caught up was she in her thoughts that the emergence of the very competent-looking girl from the interviewing office made no more than an abstracted impression on her. It was only when the receptionist said, 'Miss Sloane, Mr Peterson will see you now,' that she realised her turn had come.

Casting a swift smile at the receptionist, she came gracefully to her feet. 'Mr Peterson?'

'Right. Mr Blye Peterson.'

What's he like, this Blye Peterson? she wanted to ask. The man who holds the shape of my immediate future in his discretion, his sole discretion perhaps. But she stifled the question. Who knew but that the receptionist might take it as weakness.

Instead she paused a moment by the closed door to lift her shoulders in a show of confidence and to relax her face in a smile. It was a smile which enhanced the natural sparkle of hazel eyes and brought a glow to softly-curved cheeks. It had melted more than one man's heart, including Jonathan's, until he'd decided that what Mr Morgan's daughter Anthea offered him in the way of career success was worth more than love. Perhaps Mr Peterson would be similarly affected.

Nicola opened the door and paused in mid-step, momentarily dazzled by the sun streaming through the big glass windows. There was just an impression of light and spaciousness, of a desk with a figure behind it. And then a voice said, 'Sit down, please, Miss Sloane,' and it was low and vibrant and totally unimpressed.

Within seconds Nicola's eyes had adjusted

sufficiently to make out a chair by the desk. She walked to it, remembering to move confidently, but a sudden apprehension—could a voice affect one?—partially erased the smile from her lips.

A hand, long and lean and well shaped, reached across the table. She took it, and was aware of an odd tingling at the touch of fingers that were cool and firm. She looked across the desk, and what was left of her smile vanished.

Maleness—that was the word that hit her shocked brain. An arrogant and all-encompassing maleness. A face that was as tanned as the hand, and as well shaped, with rugged lines and gaunt angles. A chin that suggested its owner brooked no nonsense, and above it lips that were firm and strong and well defined, yet surprisingly sensuous. But it was the eyes that commanded the most attention. They were blue, a particularly vivid shade of blue. They were also alert and a little sardonic, as if her shock had been perceived.

'You're name is Nicola Sloane.' Mr Peterson had picked up a pen and was beginning to make notes on a sheet of paper in front of him. 'Age?'

'Twenty-one.'

'Young.'

'Not too young,' Nicola protested.

Blue eyes flicked her face in a look that was professionally assessing, and yet thoroughly male at the same time. 'Perhaps not,' came the brief comment. 'Status?'

'My personal information is all there in the letter I wrote,' said Nicola, a little wildly.

'So it is. Let's just say I like to hear it repeated. Status?'

'Unmarried.'

'About to be?'

'No,' Nicola said firmly.

'I see.' Again the blue eyes ran over her. Nicola wished she could read the expression in them. 'You're from Durban, I gather.'

'Yes.'

'A fair distance to travel to Nelspruit on the off chance of a job.'

'Not too far for a job I want.'

'According to your letter you've had experience in tour-guiding.'

Nicola paused only a second. 'Quite a lot.'

'Suppose,' said Blye Peterson, 'that you tell me about it.'

Eyes that had the look of being able to see to the very depths of a person's soul held hers steadily. In that moment Nicola changed her mind about lying her way through the interview.

She took a deep breath. Then she darted him a hazel-eyed smile from beneath lashes that were so thick and long that there were those who had taken them, misguidedly as it happened, to be artificial. 'Actually it's not true—I have no experience.'

The ominous expression in Blye Peterson's eyes seemed to reveal that her charm left him cold. He was about to tell her that she was wasting her time and his; that if she didn't care about her time he was extremely protective about his own. She lifted her chin, the better to meet the onslaught, and gave him another long-lashed look.

'Why did you lie?' he asked coldly.

'Because I'd never have got through this door otherwise.'

Unexpectedly the corners of his lips lifted in a grin. Nicola, who had taken Mr Peterson to be near forty, saw that he was in his early thirties, and even more attractive than she had realised.

'Well then, Miss Sloane, suppose you stop batting your eyes at me and explain why you consider yourself the right person for the position.'

Her cheeks warmed, but she said quietly, 'I'm keen and enthusiastic. I'm good with people.'

'Go on.'

'I love animals.'

'Domestic ones, no doubt.'

'Wild ones too. I admit I've no professional experience in this field, Mr Peterson, but I've spent many holidays in the game parks.'

'Ah.' A winged eyebrow lifted. 'Anything else?'

She stared at him. What more did he want?

'Nursing experience?'

'Nursing? Why no, of course not.'

'People do get sick, you know.' His tone was clipped.

'Right.' She swallowed. 'Right, they do, and they get taken to hospital.'

'This is a safari, Miss Sloane. Tour guides aren't doctors, but they do have to know enough emergency medicine to get by until the bus can reach a hospital.' He studied her a moment. 'How about survival techniques?'

'I can light a fire.'

'That's the sum total of your skills?'

Was this what was meant by third-degree questioning? Maggie had said she was foolish to apply for the job. Wise Maggie. But remorse wouldn't help her now. And she wouldn't give up without the token of a struggle.

She leaned forward in her chair, eyes sparkling with battle, any attempt at disarming him with her charm forgotten. 'You're manipulating this interview, Mr Peterson.'

'I am?' He was straight-faced.

'And it's not fair. You make me seem an idiot!'

'You read the ad, Miss Sloane. You know it stipulated experience.'

' . . . Yes.'

'You applied for an interview notwithstanding the fact that you've never guided a tour in your life.'

If he was the best-looking man she had met he must also be the most arrogant. Except for Jonathan, whose arrogance ran in another direction. Granted that what Mr Peterson said was correct, did he have to sound quite so matter-of-fact, so unutterably smug about it?

'That's true,' she acknowledged. 'I still think I deserve a chance.'

'Debatable.' Blue eyes, startlingly blue eyes against a copper tan, mocked her. But with the mockery there was also something else. Admiration? Surely not. Yet Nicola's pulses quickened.

'All right, Miss Sloane, I'll give you your chance.' He glanced at his watch. 'You have three minutes in which to convince me.'

Good of you! Nicola gritted her teeth, but in such a way that he did not see it.

'It's true I have no experience,' she began in a low voice. 'At least nothing specific. Nothing I could state in a resumé. But I *do* love wild creatures and I *am* good with people, and all my life I've dreamed of working in the outdoors.'

She looked at him and saw that his face was impassive. If she was making an impression on him she did not know it.

'Have you ever had a dream, Mr Peterson?' she asked in a sudden burst of passion.

His glance swept her, taking in the oval face with its excitement-flushed cheeks and shining eyes, the soft mouth which even in repose curved generously upward at the corners, the glossy feathered hair, so dark that it was almost black. The glance was not lost to her. So blatant was it that Nicola found herself tensing.

'Go on,' said Mr Peterson, and as Nicola expelled a breath she realised that he had not answered her question.

'I have a dream.' Her voice was husky now. 'I want to be a tour-guide—a Delayney tour-guide.' Time was running out, and she knew she had to get her point across quickly. 'I don't have formal experience, Mr Peterson, but I'm willing to learn. And I'd be a good guide. I know it! Because I'd give it everything I have.'

'You sell yourself well.' He sounded so amused that she could cheerfully have hit him.

'Then I get the job?'

'We don't make decisions without proper consideration.'

He was telling her, tactfully, that the answer was no. That the job would go to someone else— one of the girls with the tanned and wiry limbs. Nicola felt sick.

'Where can you be reached?' Blye Peterson asked.

An address to which to send the letter of refusal, politely worded: Dear Miss Sloane, we regret that we are unable to avail ourselves of your services. If you should care to contact us again at some future time. . . . Polite hogwash.

Discarding all caution—what was there left to

lose at this point?—she sat forward, poised on the edge of her chair. Like a graceful bird ready for flight, thought the watching man.

'I mean to be a tour-guide, Mr Peterson,' she declared. 'Nothing will hold me back. Nothing at all.'

Blue eyes narrowed, but 'Can we reach you at your Durban address?' was all he said. Clearly her determination had made no impact on him. For a moment Nicola wondered if she had made a fool of herself, then decided she did not care.

'You can reach me here in Nelspruit.' She gave him the name of the motel.'

'You're not going back right away, then?'

'Not till I hear from you.'

'Miss Sloane.' Mr Peterson put the pen down and looked at her, a level look that sent a tremor quivering through her. 'I hope you haven't spent a lot of money coming here. After all, you must have known your chances were just about nil.'

A lot? A fool's amount, Maggie had said, and she was right. What with the cost of the motel and meals, not to mention the plane ticket, she had almost used up her savings. But you don't need to know that, Mr all-powerful Peterson, with your handsome face and your expensive clothes. Just as you don't need to know my disappointment because your last words have made it clear that all of it was in vain.

Smiling brightly, Nicola said, 'Heavens, no, I could well afford it.'

A speculative look from those very perceptive eyes. Something slightly amused in a face that was compellingly male. He knows, Nicola thought. Oh, but that's impossible. I'm letting the arrogance of the man get the better of me.

'I can afford it,' she said again, on a higher note.

'I'm glad to hear it.' The tone was impersonal. 'I think that's it, then, Miss Sloane. We'll let you know one way or the other.'

The sun blazed down from a cloudless sky, turning the wide streets of Nelspruit to dazzles of shimmering tar. Lining the sidewalks were jacarandas and poinsettias, but Nicola hardly noticed them.

'We'll let you know one way or the other,' Mr Peterson had said. The expression in those steel-blue eyes had made it clear that he knew already which way the decision would go.

There was no point, really, in remaining in Nelspruit to await a call the contents of which she knew already. She might as well go back to Durban. In fact the sooner she did so the better, for she must find a new job and the salary that would go with it.

Maggie had been right, as always. Darling Maggie, who possessed none of Nicola's impulsiveness and did not understand it. Faced with the humiliation of being jilted in favour of a rich girl, Maggie would have swallowed her fury and set about reorganising her life in a sensible and matter-of-fact way. She would not have spent near to her last penny in chasing a job for which she had no qualifications. Yes, Maggie had been right, but little comfort that knowledge was at this point.

Nicola paused to kick a stone into a hedge. The small explosion of energy was some release for her feelings. She gave a laugh that was half a sob, and looked around her, really looked, for the first time. Chances were she might never come here again, and she had paid a night's board, there was no point in leaving till tomorrow. Silly not to explore. The fact that she might miss Mr Peterson's call gave her no pause for qualms. She knew what he would say—this was one call not worth waiting for.

As she lifted her head to the sun, letting it warm her face, she felt a lightening of her spirits. The interview had left her more tense than she had realised. It was not only the interview itself, and the need to defend her lack of wisdom in applying for the job, that had been a strain. In some strange way Mr Peterson had set her nerves tingling, and she did not know why. Would never know, for she would not see him again. She lifted her chin a fraction higher.

Sun-drenched and sparkling, Nelspruit was even prettier than she had realised. It was a place of colour. All manner of reds crowded and clashed in parks and gardens, with flashes of yellow and orange adding to the general bright-ness. The streets were wide, for the city fathers of a forgotten era had considered the ox-wagons which must be able to execute complete turns. There was the sound of bird-song and the air was fragrant. Nicola examined a flowered sundial on a lawn before the City Hall, then spotted a fruit stall where she spent five minutes trying to choose between peaches and mangoes that were big and glossy and pear-shaped. Settling for mangoes, she found a small park, and in the shade of a flame-tree, she bit into the flesh of a fruit that was so sweet and succulent that the gods might well have called it ambrosia.

A lizard slithered over a rock, and from a

nearby bed of red poppies came the incessant drone of bees. It was quiet here, and so beautiful. Perfidious Jonathan and his Anthea Morgan seemed a long way away. The interview was forgotten. Well—almost forgotten. As for the disturbing Mr Peterson, he would soon be a memory. Nicola realised suddenly that she was smiling. Making the most of the day had been a splendid idea.

The sun was setting when she finally made her way back to the motel. She opened the door of her room to the sound of a ringing phone.

'Miss Sloane?' The voice, low and spine-tinglingly gravelly, was amazingly familiar after such short acquaintance. 'Where've you been? I was about to give up on you.'

Did you think I'd sit around waiting for your duty call? I had better things to do than that.

She opened her mouth to speak, when she heard him say, 'I thought I'd have to offer the job to someone else instead.'

Nicola felt the blood drain from her cheeks. The hand that held the phone, as tightly as if it was a slippery object that would slip from her grip, was white-knuckled.

'You're giving me the job?'

'If you still want it.' The low voice was amused. 'Your absence seemed to indicate that you'd changed your mind.'

'Oh, I want it!' she breathed.

There were a few moments of silence. Then Blye Peterson said, 'Your first safari departs on the twenty-fifth.'

Nicola did a rapid calculation. Almost a month.

'You'll have to attend a training session first, starting a week earlier.'

That meant returning to Durban, coming back again to Nelspruit. Eating. Living. More calculations.

'Could I start sooner?'

In an altered voice, the man at the other end of the line said, 'There is an earlier trip. And a training session beginning day after tomorrow.'

'I'll take it,' said Nicola, very quickly, without thought.

This time the silence at the other end of the line was longer. Then Blye Peterson said, 'So you did spend unwisely.'

Nicola felt her cheeks warm, and was glad he could not see them. '. . . A little.'

'More than a little, I'd say.'

Did the man have to have his pound of flesh?

'Does it matter?'

'It's the second time you've lied to me.' His tone was smooth as butter.

Nicola was thinking of a retort when he added, 'Let's have the truth between us in future, Miss Sloane.'

Nicola, to whom falsehood was normally abhorrent—her two deviations therefrom had seemed necessary and could surely not be called lies—found it easy to say yes. Besides, she thought there was no 'future' to speak of. Delayney Tours was a huge concern. Blye Peterson was a member of the personnel department, Nicola would be a tour-guide. It was unlikely that they would see each other again. The knowledge brought an irritating pang of disappointment. So what if Blye Peterson was the most striking-looking man she had met? Jonathan had been good-looking too—in a different, weaker way—and her absorption in him had given her nothing but grief. She was embarking on a new career. Nicola Sloane, tour-guide—the very words were a thrill. Men would be the farthest thing from her mind.

'I won't lie to you again,' she promised.

Nicola enjoyed every minute of the training session—the wide open spaces, the rustic atmosphere of the game park, the cooking fires and the taste of barbecued meat, the sounds and smells of the bushveld. Learning about animals, about the flora of the region. Learning how to cope with the emergencies which could arise when one was some distance from the facilities of the nearest city.

One afternoon, late, as the sun was setting, she stood by the wire fence of the camp where the session was being conducted, and looked across the river and the bush. To the untrained eye there would be only the bush and the deserted river, but even after a few days Nicola was able to pick up signs that she would not have noticed before. Less than a hundred yards away some buck were making their way to the water. She could just make out a hint of movement, the flash of brown that was not quite the colour of the trees. The buck were moving slowly. Perhaps she would catch sight of them as they emerged from the scrub on to the muddy bank of the river, perhaps the light would have vanished by then and it would be too dark to see. No matter; there would be other buck—many of them. Other animals. Her lips lifted in a smile of contentment.

Blye Peterson had been right. There was much a tour-guide had to know, and no doubt the other applicants had known it all. But he had given her the job—had he thought she would wither with despair if he did not?—and now she was determined to learn as much as she could.

Unbidden his image entered her mind, crowding out the buck and the colours of the sunset. As if he was standing beside her at the camp fence, she could see his face, the vivid eyes, the strong lines of his cheeks and nose and chin, the air of rugged gauntness.

His last words came back to her. 'Let's have the truth between us in future, Miss Sloane,' and she knew the sound of his voice, could actually hear the vibrant timbre. It was strange that he had made quite such an impact on her.

With some effort she banished his face from her mind and concentrated instead, very hard, on the ephemeral shapes of the buck. Men had no place in her life for the present. She was going to be a career woman, a tour-guide, and she was determined that she would be a good one. Blye Peterson would be proud that he had hired her. Darn! She had thought of the man again. How did he keep inserting himself into her thoughts? *She* would be proud of *herself*.

The zest which had once gone into her work at Morgan's Agricultural now went into preparing herself for her new career. She hung on the instructor's every word, and at night, when the day's work was done, she sat up till late, poring over animal literature by the light of a kerosene lamp.

The session over, it was back to Nelspruit, and the start of a worrying period. There were still a few days to go before the departure of the safari, and Nicola's funds were almost depleted. The owner of the motel had looked exceedingly glum when she'd pleaded with him to wait for payment of her room until she received her first salary cheque. There was also the matter of meals.

The safari was to start on Friday, and by Wednesday Nicola was worrying in earnest. Financially she was almost at rock bottom. In the offices of Delayney Tours that morning she could think of nothing else. She had come in for her uniforms, had put one on to make sure that the fit was correct, but with her problems weighing her down she had not even looked at herself.

What would be the reaction if she were to ask for a loan? The training instructor, an understanding woman with a sense of humour, was not at the office, and the girl who had fitted her with the uniforms had no authority. There was the receptionist. Nicola glanced at the girl, even nerved herself to take a few steps towards her, then stopped. Well-groomed and bland, the girl looked as if she did not know what it was to be hungry. At most she could liaise between Nicola and the person empowered to make financial decisions. But would she be prepared to? Nicola took another step towards her then stopped, for at the end of the corridor she had seen a figure she recognised.

Her grandmother, bless her indomitable soul, had been an avid believer in omens. Unless Nicola was vastly mistaken, one had just now presented itself to her.

'Miss Sloane!' the receptionist was calling after Nicola as she made her way swiftly towards him. She was saying that unauthorised personnel were not allowed in this corridor, but Nicola did not hear her.

'Mr Peterson!'

He turned and looked down at her, the rugged face set in a slight frown. He was so tall Nicola thought, looking up at him—taller by far than she'd realised. The only time she had seen him he had been seated behind a desk.

'Nicola Sloane.' The rugged face cleared. 'And looking the picture of a tour-guide in that smart safari suit.'

His voice had none of the matter-of-factness of the interview, and he was smiling. Nicola was flooded with a sudden and intense happiness. For a moment, as she thanked him for the compliment, even her worries were forgotten.

'When do you start?' he asked.

'Friday.' She took a deep breath for courage. 'I need a favour rather badly. I don't know whom to ask. May I talk to you, Mr Peterson?'

'Sure. Come in here.'

CHAPTER TWO

ALMOST where they stood was a door which he opened. Nicola followed him inside, and even through her apprehension she saw at once that this office was far removed from the one where she had had her interview. On the door she had glimpsed the name Delayney, and the room befitted the man whom she could only suppose was the Chairman of the big corporation that was Delayney Tours. The walls were pannelled in a sleekly pale mahogany, the carpet was thick and plush underfoot. Desk and chairs were long-lined and elegant, and there were several lovely pictures.

'Well?'

At the word her eyes left the furnishings of the room and she turned.

'Well?' Mr Peterson asked again. His eyes had a sparkle and his lips were lifted at the corners. Nicola found herself wondering how those lips would feel on her own. A moment later, realising the drift of her thoughts, she was horrified. She had enough problems without looking for new ones!

'I was wondering,' she said, 'if I could have an advance on my first month's salary.' Giving him no time to reply, she rushed on. 'I realise you're not the person to ask—but I don't know who to approach.'

'I can organise it for you.' His expression as he studied her was so speculative that she felt warmth rush to her cheeks. 'You really did take a chance, didn't you?'

It was not easy to retain her dignity. 'You already know that,' she said stiffly.

She thought he would counter the comment, but he did not. To her surprise he drew a cheque-book from a pocket, opened it and began to write.

'Enough?' he asked, handing her the cheque.

'More than enough,' she said gratefully. 'I didn't think you could do this. I mean, you're really in Personnel, aren't you?'

'There are things I can do,' he responded easily. And then, on a new note, 'Do you often take chances?'

His tone had a teasing quality that was oddly seductive. Nicola's heart did an alarming leap. 'When something means very much to me, then yes, I do,' she said, a little unsteadily. Recklessly she added, 'You're a chancer too.'

He looked intrigued. 'I am?'

'You've just given me a cheque without any authority. And as for this office'—she glanced around her—'what on earth would Mr Delayney say if he knew you were here?'

If Blye Peterson was at all discomfited he did not show it. 'What indeed? So you'd say we're both chancers, then?'

His eyes were a vivid blue against the tan. When he smiled the rugged features took on a rakish air that enhanced his good looks. Women must fall around him like leaves around a tree. Involuntarily Nicola wondered if he was married.

The smile broadened infectiously. Never one for the small formalities of life, Nicola forgot her dignity. She laughed, the sound joyous in a room whose elegance seemed to denote that wealthy corporate beings were its usual occupants. 'Both chancers? Most definitely,' she agreed.

'We have something in common, then. Did you enjoy the training session?'

'Every minute of it.'

'Learn a lot?'

'So much.' She darted him a quizzical look. 'Did you know that an elephant's trunk can weigh as much as three hundred pounds?'

'No! It does?'

'Absolutely.'

'I didn't realise the sessions went into quite so much detail.'

His teeth were very white, and when he grinned the high cheekbones were emphasised. Women who thought Robert Redford was sexy hadn't met Blye Peterson!

'Oh, they don't.' Nicola was unaware of quite the extent to which her own smile transfigured her appearance, unaware that the watching man thought the soft natural blush and glowing eyes turned loveliness to beauty. 'I read that in a book. I've read three books about animals since I saw you last, and I've filled a whole book with notes.'

Strangely, Mr Peterson did not immediately respond. Instead he looked at her in a way that sent her pulses racing. Swallowing hard on a lump in her throat, Nicola forced herself to remain very still beneath his scrutiny.

'This job really does mean a lot to you,' he said at last.

'Very much,' she acknowledged softly.

'I'm glad,' he said, and somehow the words were unexpected.

Why did you hire me? she wanted to ask. Why me, when the other applicants were all more experienced? Her lips parted, the question trembling on her tongue but she stilled it. They had agreed that she was a chancer, but there was no sense in her chancing her luck when it wasn't necessary. No wisdom in it at all. Despite the fact that not a day had gone by since the interview when she did not wonder at the answer.

'You have a question?' she heard him ask.

'No.'

'Then I'll just wish you luck and say goodbye.'

She shook the hand he reached out to her. It was firm and cool, a strong hand. Somehow, she forced herself to smile. It was ridiculous that she should feel quite so disappointed at the knowledge that she would not see him again. Utterly ridiculous. Her smile deepened. Not for anything would she let him know her sense of loss.

Nicola was up at daybreak on the first day of the safari. In her pyjamas she ran to the window, flung it open and looked outside. With the sun just a promise in the east, it was still too dark to see much, but the sky seemed clear enough and the air had the lovely sweet-smelling freshness of the semi-tropics. It would be a good day, she decided, a clear omen that the trip was going to be a success.

It took a few minutes for the cold to penetrate her excitement. Later, when the sun had risen, it would be very hot, but now chill air filled the room from the open window. Nicola curled her bare toes and wrapped her arms around herself. Below her, in the motel garden, shrubs that she remembered as being flamboyantly scarlet were an indefinable grey mass, and a cat slinking its way back from some nocturnal rendezvous was little more than a fast-moving shape. It was very quiet. Even the travelling salesmen, usually on the road early, were not yet about. Clearly most sensible people were still abed.

Glancing at her watch, Nicola knew she had at least an hour before she had to think of getting ready. Yet sleep was impossible—she was far too excited.

The room boasted a small stove and kitchen essentials, and she had laid in a stock of supplies to obviate going to restaurants. In no time the kettle was boiling. As she drank her coffee she wondered about the day that lay ahead.

Too restless to go back to bed, she showered, washed her hair, and put on the new safari suit. The sun rises quickly in the South African Lowveld. By the time Nicola was dressed the room was light enough for her to see her reflection in the mirror. Not one to dwell on her appearance, she was glad nevertheless with what she saw. The make-up she had applied was hardly necessary, for her eyes sparkled with anticipation and her skin was a light golden tan from the week in the sun. The safari suit was a perfect fit, the belt hugging a trim waist, the sleek cut revealing a figure that was both slender yet gently curved. Two days ago, at the offices of Delayney Tours, she had given the minimum of attention to the safari suit; there had been more pressing problems on her mind. For the first time she saw how smart it was, how well it fitted her.

'Nicola Sloane, tour-guide,' she said aloud to the reflection in the mirror. And as she turned away she was glad that Blye Peterson had seen her in her uniform.

She was at the bus depot well before time. A neat folder held her papers. John Bailey was the name of the driver. She had not met him yet, but was told he would arrive shortly, as would the members of the tour. Nicola's excitement increased by the minute.

In the event, the passengers arrived before the driver. Nicola, who had spent hours browsing over her register, felt she hardly needed to consult her clip-board to identify them. As they arrived in ones and twos, twenty people in all, instinct told her who many of them were.

She smiled as she greeted them. 'Welcome to Delayney Tours. I hope your tour will be a memorable one.' She gave each person a folder with particulars of the trip.

'Thank you,' was the formal reply of a young couple, Mr and Mrs Anton Mavroni, honeymooners by their appearance, Italian by their accent: the husband was thin and a little nervous, the wife sloe-eyed and quite beautiful.

'I've looked forward to this for so long,' said Mrs Barnes, an elderly lady with a sweet face. Nicola saw that she dragged a leg when she walked and that she held a cane. She made a mental note that the front seat, which had the most leg-room, would be reserved for her.

There was an American couple, by the name of Slade. Handsome-looking people, with big cameras slung across their shoulders. 'Jim and May,' they introduced themselves.

'I hope you'll get some good shots,' Nicola offered, warming to their easy informality.

'That would be great,' said Bill. 'Must have something to show the guys back home!'

Still they came. Men and women, some a little

formal, all friendly, all looking forward to the
days ahead. Apart from the honeymooners, the
youngest member of the tour was Derek
Marsden, a gangling man with a curly mop of red
hair and laughing eyes, much the same age as
herself, Nicola thought. He gave her an assessing
look as she handed him her folder. It was a look
that was all male, yet so cheekily friendly with it,
that Nicola could not help but grin back at him.

'I'll have to sit near you,' he said with an
appealing grin.

'This is a safari, not a dating game. And I'm
your guide,' she told him, but without rancour.
'The bus is filling up, Mr Marsden, why don't
you find yourself a seat.'

'Derek, please,' he countered cheerfully. 'When
do we leave, Nicola? I may call you Nicola, I
suppose?'

'Oh yes, everyone will do that.' She frowned
down at her list. 'We should leave any time now.
We're just waiting for one more passenger, Mrs
Gloria Payne.' The name had been added in pen
to the bottom of the typed list; evidently Mrs
Payne had made a last-minute reservation. 'And
then there's the driver. I wonder where he is.'

'Right here,' said a familiar voice that sent
shock-waves through her system.

Spinning round, Nicola gasped, 'You!'

He looked so different from the other times she
had seen him. Then Blye Peterson had been
dressed formally in suit and tie. Now he wore a
safari suit similar to Nicola's own cream-coloured
one, the cut of it revealing arms and legs and
throat that were tanned and muscular.

'I don't understand,' she said unsteadily.

'I'm your driver.'

'You can't be!' Still in shock, she glanced at the clip-board.' 'It says here John Bailey.'

'I've taken his place,' said Blye Peterson crisply. 'And here,' he gestured, 'is your last passenger.'

It must have been the measure of her shock, Nicola thought, that she had not registered the woman who stood at Blye Peterson's side. Gloria Payne was as glorious as her name implied. Tall and voluptuous, with hair a golden blonde that fell in curls so stylishly casual that only an expensive hairdresser could have achieved quite that effect. The emerald slacks suit was as stylish as the rest of her. There was something very proprietorial in her closeness to Mr Peterson. Nicola disliked her on sight.

Perhaps because she was aware of the injustice of her feelings Nicola's manner to this last passenger was particularly friendly. 'We're so glad to have you with us, Mrs Payne. We hope you'll have a good time.'

The answering smile from beneath mascaraed lashes was directed at Mr Peterson. 'I'm certain I'll have a marvellous time. Coming, Blye?'

'In a moment. I suggest you do as Nicola suggests and find yourself a seat.'

Nicola watched Gloria Payne climb into the bus, long-legged and languidly graceful, and then she turned to the man at her side. 'Mr Peterson, I really don't understand. . . .'

'There'll be time to talk later.' His voice was matter-of-fact but his grin wicked. 'On safari we don't stand on ceremony, Nicola. The name is Blye.'

As she boarded the bus, Blye behind her, Nicola was immediately aware of tension. Mrs

Barnes shifted uneasily in her front seat. Gloria Payne standing above her, wore an imperious look that made a beautiful face very hard.

'Is there a problem?' Nicola asked.

'It's ridiculous.' Gloria Payne looked past her, just as if she did not exist, at Blye. 'I thought I'd sit here.'

'The seat is taken,' Nicola said politely. 'There's one left farther down.'

'I can see that.' The other woman was impatient. 'This is the one I want.'

'I can move.' Mrs Barnes was flushed and unhappy, obviously upset at being the focus of attention.

There was silence in the bus, as if every one of the passengers awaited the outome of the altercation. Nicola was aware that behind her Blye was as still as the others.

She had not expected the first test to come quite so soon. She knew she had to rise to it. 'That won't be necessary,' she told Mrs Barnes quietly.

'She offered.' This from Gloria Payne, and Mrs Barnes said, 'I really don't mind.'

'You'll be more comfortable where you are.' Nicola kept her composure.

'Blye. . . .' Gloria Payne appealed to the man who stood at the driver's wheel.

Don't let him answer. Don't let him undermine my authority. If he does, the passengers will have no respect for me. And I will have lost my respect for him.

'*I* am in charge of this side of things, Mrs Payne,' Nicola said firmly. 'Now I would appreciate it if you would kindly take your seat, as we're ready to go.'

Gloria Payne threw one last look at Blye. Nicola could not see his face, but she saw Gloria's, and her expression was strange, pointed—almost as if she knew something that Nicola did not.

Blye remained silent, and after a moment Gloria turned. Sending a look of pure venom in Nicola's direction—she angled it in such a way that only Nicola would have been able to see it— she made for the back seat.

Nicola expelled a breath she had not known she was holding and relaxed the fingers that had been curled into her palms. She saw that Derek Marsden was mouthing her a silent 'Well done!' Picking up her microphone, she smiled and extended a collective welcome to the passengers. 'My name is Nicola and I'm your tour-guide,' she told them. 'Our driver is Blye. We hope the trip will be an enjoyable one for you all.'

As they took the road out of the town and towards the game-park Nicola spoke several times, giving names to the flora that lined the way; the lovely poinsettia, the azaleas and the flame-trees. She spoke briefly about the crops in the fields beyond, the citrus and the tobacco for which the area was famous. But she made it a point to keep her patter to a minimum. It was an insult to anyone's intelligence, the instructor had said, to feed people with the obvious.

Shortly before arriving at the park gates Blye stopped the bus and Nicola told the group that those wanting coffee or bathroom facilities should make use of the opportunity. Once they entered the park there would be no getting out of the bus until they were in camp.

When Blye took the wheel once more there was a feeling of excitement in the bus. Cameras were everywhere, and many of the passengers sat forward, their eyes on the passing landscape. Only Gloria looked a little bored. Nicola wondered what had brought her on the trip. Involuntarily she turned and glanced at Blye.

She had been glad to see him—no denying that—but his presence made her tense too. The circumstances of his presence here were so strange. Blye was in Personnel, and what had happened to John Bailey? He sat loose and lithe in the driver's seat, handling the bus with the easy competence of one who did this job every day. Which he did not. What, Nicola wondered, was he doing here? Blye Peterson had some explaining to do!

And then they were entering the park, and as they drove through the stone gates bordered with proteas and covered with purple bougainvillaea, Nicola stopped thinking of Blye. They were in the game park. Her job had begun, really begun. Now she was really Nicola Sloane, tour-guide. Microphone in hand, she began to tell the passengers a little of what they could expect to see.

They had driven no more than fifteen minutes when Nicola was alerted by a flash of brown. It was a colour that was not unlike the shades of the bush, and before her training she might not have noticed it, for it was a little way from the road.

Leaning forward, she touched Blye's shoulder. 'I see something.'

He brought the bus to a stop, and there was a buzz of excitement from the group as Nicola gestured. Let it be worthwhile, she prayed, knowing that the first animal is always one of the most memorable on any safari.

'What is it?' the passengers wanted to know as they peered through the windows, cameras at the ready.

For the moment there was just a dab of brown. First day out on the training session Nicola had sometimes mistaken anthills for animals. A common mistake, the supervisor had soothed, but one to be avoided if possible. With relief she saw some movement against the trees. An animal, no doubt about that, but it was far from the road and well camouflaged.

'Are we going to stop for every one of Nicola's false alarms?' Gloria's voice at the back of the bus was petulant.

Nobody took any notice of her. Not even Blye. Starting the bus, he edged it slowly forward, very slowly, not more than a metre or so. As he drew to a silent halt there was a collective gasp from the passengers who could see from a new angle, and there really was an animal, possibly a big one.

'Now what?' Nicola breathed.

Blye switched off the ignition. 'We'll just wait here for a while.'

'You don't mind?'

He turned to her, his eyes amused. 'You're the guide.'

It seemed she could not look at him without sensation, the strangest quiver, she had never experienced anything quite like it.

'I'd like to wait.' Softly, so that the passengers could not hear her, she added, 'And it's true, I am a guide. This morning I looked in the mirror and said, "Nicola Sloane, tour-guide", but even then I think I hardly believed it.'

'Now?' His expression had altered a fraction, the amusement tinged with something else, something Nicola could not quite define. It made no sense that her heart should beat faster.

'I believe it.'

There were exclamations from the passengers. Blye turned to the window. 'Your beast is making itself known, Nicola.'

It was moving, walking in the direction of the road. Quite suddenly it emerged from the bush. A giraffe, long neck sloping, head daintily aloof, graciously beautiful.

Pausing, it surveyed the bus a moment before turning disdainfully to a tall acacia to nibble at its leaves. Cameras clicked and whirred.

Nicola's eye was caught by more movement. 'There's another one!' she exclaimed. 'The mate, I expect. With luck we'll see it too.'

They did. Just a minute later and the two giraffes were together, as if they had not seen each other for a while, their necks inclined in greeting, one long neck twined gracefully against the other. In the bus the cameras worked furiously. And then the giraffes drew apart and concentrated on the trees.

'Ready to go?' Blye asked after a while.

'Just a few minutes more,' Nicola begged on a burst of intuition.

Elated, she watched as two more giraffes emerged from the bush. Little ones these were, babies, with none of the disdainful dignity possessed by their elders. In playful mood they strayed towards the road, legs moving in a strange loping movement that was simultaneously awkward and graceful.

Nicola was no less enraptured than the

passengers. Involuntarily she laughed. The sound was buoyant, its joy as unrestrained as the animals she watched. In that moment she was forgetful of her status as tour-guide, totally unaware that more than one person—and two men in particular—thought her laugh the loveliest they had heard.

The baby giraffes cantered some way down the road before making for the bush at the other side. At a slower pace their parents followed. Blye took the bus forward, following the movement till the animals were well in the bush and out of sight.

'Fantastic!' called Jim Slade, and Mrs Barnes said, 'Oh, that was just lovely!'

Nicola barely heard them. She only had ears for Blye's murmured, 'Well spotted!'

The bus began to move. On a sigh of happiness Nicola turned to the window and the now deserted bush. It had been an auspicious beginning.

As Nicola knocked on the door of the bungalow her heart was beating uncomfortably fast. Idiot, she told herself fiercely. You're here purely on a matter of business, there's no need to feel quite so nervous.

There was a shouted 'Come inside,' and she opened the door.

Blye had his back to her. He had on the safari shorts he had worn earlier, but his feet were bare and he was naked from the waist up. He was towelling himself. His hair was wet, and a back that was even more muscular than Nicola had imagined it would be was damp and bronzed. The breath skittered in her throat.

'I hadn't expected you yet,' he said without turning.

She hadn't known that he was expecting her at all. 'I can come back later.' It was an effort to speak.

At her words he spun round, and his eyebrows lifted in surprise. 'Nicola!'

'It *is* early. I'm sorry, I should have guessed you'd be freshening up.'

He took a step towards her. 'What are you doing here?'

'You said. . . .' She stopped, her throat suddenly dry. 'It wasn't me you were expecting.'

He took another step forward. He was all vibrant masculinity. She had never seen anyone quite like him. His shoulders were very broad, his hips tapered. Shamelessly her gaze went to his bare legs, taut and muscled as the rest of him, then back to his arms and chest to which hair clung dark and wet.

The room was a carbon copy of her own, which she had not considered small. Yet suddenly she felt that she could push the walls aside with her hands. Such was the power of his maleness that it seemed to fill the room, dwarfing whatever was in it.

His face was very rugged, and eyes that she had seen warm and amused, glinted. 'What are you doing here?' he asked again.

I must have been totally crazy. I should have known the effect you'd have on me. You certainly know it.

She swallowed. 'We'll talk later.'

She was about to leave when she found her hands seized in his, keeping her there. Her heart gave a funny little lurch. 'Blye. . . .'

'You couldn't wait to see me alone. Well, Nicola, what is it? Come for a kiss?'

'Don't flatter yourself!'

'Am I?' He laughed, the sound husky and low and fire to her maddened nerves. Without warning he pulled her against him. He held her loosely but very still. She could feel the long length of him against her, the bare chest just an inch from her cheeks, the taut legs touching hers. He made no move to kiss her. In a way she wished that he would, for this taut motionless grip was more sensuous, more unnerving, than any kiss could have been.

'Yes,' she said into his chest, 'you . . . you do flatter yourself.'

He laughed again. 'Then why are you trembling?'

Somehow she managed to tilt back her head. He was so close to her that she could see the little lines around his eyes and lips. 'I like to choose my company, that's why. Let me go, Blye.'

Unexpectedly he did. Head spinning, she was turning to the door when she felt a hand on her waist. 'Why did you come?' he asked softly.

'To find out why you took John Bailey's place.'

'I see,' he said after a moment.

'Perhaps you think it shouldn't matter to me, but it did.'

'Did?'

'It did then—when I saw you at the bus this morning.'

'And now it doesn't matter any longer?'

'No,' she lied.

'I see,' he said once more. And then, 'John was ill.'

'Couldn't he have been replaced with another driver?'

'He could.'

'Well then?'

He was still very close to her. Despite her anger it was hard not to look at him. He was so handsome. No, handsome was not the right word. He was gaunt and rugged and the lines of his face were too stern for conventional good looks. Yet somehow, for all of that, he was the most attractive man she had met.

'I like to do different things,' Blye explained. 'I've been wanting to drive a safari.'

'Just for the hell of it.' She was not sure why she sounded so angry.

'Just for the hell of it,' he agreed. A hand reached out and touched her chin, the fingers stroked her throat. She could not escape, she was already backed up against the door. She stood very still. Not for anything did she want him to know that inside her she was exploding with excitement.

'You should find that easy to understand,' he went on softly.

'Me?' The word emerged of its own accord, she was too giddy to think coherently.

'Yes, you, Nicola. You said we were both chancers. Is it so odd that we should both like a change of occupation as well?'

'Maybe not.' The blur was clearing just a little. 'But there's something we don't have in common, Blye Peterson. You're out for easy flirtatiousness; I'm not.'

'In my experience many women are.'

She looked at him, caught by a harshness she did not understand. 'Perhaps,' she said slowly, 'you've met the wrong woman.'

'Perhaps.'

No wonder, really. She had thought the first time she saw him that women would be drawn to him. She was herself. No, that was not true. She was intrigued by him, fascinated by a personality that was stronger and more sexual than any she had ever encountered. It could not be more than that.

'I have to go now,' she said in a choked voice. And then, one hand on the door handle, she could not resist asking, 'You seemed to be expecting someone when I came in.'

He looked down at her without answering. His lips were curved slightly at the corners, his eyes were enigmatic. He seemed puzzled by a naïvety that was strange to him.

A second later Nicola realised why. The answer that popped into her mind was so simple that she wondered why she had not known it all the time.

'Gloria?'

'Gloria,' he agreed evenly.

Over the quite unjustified pain in her chest, Nicola said lightly, 'It's early. Just half an hour since I got everybody settled. Don't give up on her yet.'

'I won't.' She heard the mockery in his tone as she closed the door with a slight bang.

She had taken no more than fifty steps when a graceful figure appeared through the trees—none other than Gloria, walking towards Blye's bungalow. Nicola paused in mid-step. She should not be surprised, not after what had just happened. Nor should she feel disappointed. Blye's personal life had nothing to do with her. She did not care about it one way or the other, she told herself.

It was surely not her duty to stop to talk to Gloria. She made to turn direction.

Too late. Gloria had seen her, had turned too, was obviously coming her way.

'Nicola!'

'Hello, Mrs Payne. Your accommodation is all right, I hope?'

'Perfect. Why the formality?'

'Gloria,' Nicola amended, hating her. Gloria had changed into another slacks suit. The cut was long and sleek, the appearance expensive, as if she had walked into a stylish boutique, one that had a special range called 'Safari'.

'You don't observe the same formality with our Blye.' Gloria's tone was easy.

Nicola was caught off guard. 'What do you mean?'

'If I'm not mistaken that was his bungalow you've just come from.'

'You're not mistaken.'

'Couldn't wait to get your hands on him?'

Blye's line of thought exactly. A furious retort sprang to Nicola's lips, but she managed to suppress it. Even in her anger she knew she had to be careful. As a representative of Delayney Tours she must be polite to one of its guests. The customer is always right, even when she is wrong. She gritted her teeth.

'I'm afraid in that you *are* mistaken,' she said with icy politeness. 'Blye and I had things to discuss—safari business.'

'Well, aren't you efficient! Not half an hour in camp and already you're involved with details.'

'Correct. And as I have a few more to attend to I'll be on my way.'

'In a moment.' A gorgeously-manicured hand touched her arm. 'I think I should tell you that Blye can eat little girls at one sitting.'

Nicola's patience had its limits. 'Then you shouldn't have anything to worry about,' she returned equably.

'How dare you!' There was no missing the venom in Gloria's face. 'Delayney Tours will hear of your insolence! Blye too.'

'No insolence was intended.' Nicola kept her feelings concealed behind a blank mask. 'You're a very beautiful and sophisticated woman. I'd have thought the last thing you'd want was to be thought of as a little girl.'

Without waiting for an answer, she walked on. Her eyes were on the path, she was blind to the flame trees that brightened the camp garden, to the mischievous blue jays that squabbled on the ground. The joy had gone out of the day. She wished Gloria Payne had chosen another tour. She wished John Bailey had not been taken ill.

CHAPTER THREE

NICOLA did not brood long. It was not in her nature to do so, and besides, there was much to keep her busy. She was determined to make a success of the job, and she took her new duties very seriously.

She was checking the barbecues when Derek Marsden came up to her. He was nice, she thought, noticing again the untidy red hair, the boyish grin. At his 'Hi there, Nicola,' she couldn't help grinning back.

'Glad to see you smiling,' he said.

'Shouldn't I be?'

'I hoped you wouldn't let the viper get to you.'

She stared at him. 'Gloria Payne?'

'None other,' he chuckled.

'You overheard!' she accused, wondering who else had heard the interchange and what they had made of it.

'Couldn't help it. Vicious hag!'

'She isn't exactly pleasant. She. . . .' Nicola stopped in confusion, covering her mouth with her hand. 'Heavens, I shouldn't be talking like this!'

'Why not?'

'You're both passengers. I'm the guide.'

'You're still human.' His grin was irrepressible. 'A very lovely human too.'

'I was beginning to wonder.' Her eyes warmed with a sparkle she was unable to suppress. 'You're a flirt, Derek.'

'Oh, now come, I'm saying no more than the truth.' His grin deepened. 'I intend to say it often.'

Fast worker, she thought, but she wasn't angry. It would be hard to be angry with Derek. Besides, his frank appreciation of her was doing much to restore her confidence.

'Ready to go out?' she asked him, changing the subject. 'There's time for a drive before dusk. I'm going to start rounding up the group.'

By the time Nicola stood by the bus, waiting for the passengers to get on, she felt much more cheerful. It was unfortunate that Gloria Payne was on this safari, her first one. But here and there she would meet up with other Glorias. In the course of her interview she had told Blye that she liked people, that she felt she could deal with them. It was up to her to deal with Gloria, and she would.

Blye Peterson was another matter. She tried not to think of him.

Looking virile and powerful, he took his seat at the driver's wheel; his safari suit was immaculate, and fitted so well that it might have been custom-made for him, yet Nicola found herself looking through the cream-coloured fabric, seeing him as he had been in the bungalow. Semi-nude, bronzed and muscular, his body had reminded her of Greek sculptures she had seen in art books.

She looked up and caught his eyes. They were narrowed, more than a little mocking. He knew what she was thinking. Without a word being said, he *knew*. Nicola lifted her chin.

'Ready?' she asked coolly, when all the passengers had boarded.

'Ready—and willing.' He said it so blandly that Nicola had no need to wonder if the double entendre had been intended. Her cheeks flamed, and she heard him chuckle.

'What about you?' he went on.

'Ready to give of my best.' She responded so quietly that only Blye could have heard. And make of that what you want, she thought fiercely.

Without waiting to see his reaction she turned to the passengers and gave them her most brilliant smile. 'We'll be driving along the river,' she told them. 'I see you all have your cameras with you. Let's hope you'll have occasion to use them!'

The atmosphere on the bus was generally more relaxed than it had been. People were starting to talk to each other, to make friends. Only Gloria kept herself aloof. Nicola wondered why she thought herself special.

The river road had been Nicola's choice, Blye had fallen in with her suggestion. She wondered whether the group noticed that he had the look of a man who gave orders, important ones. Perhaps they did not, for if in a well-cut grey suit he had the air of being used to making decisions in a corporate boardroom—odd that, for it was obviously not where he belonged—then the air of tanned virility made him seem equally at home in the wilderness of the game park.

Gloria was impressed with him, that much was apparent. There was a hunger in the woman's eyes when she looked at him. It was a look that made Nicola feel uncomfortable. The next tour, she thought, had to be easier. No longer would she be a novice, and neither Gloria nor Blye would be present to upset her equilibrium.

The road had been well chosen. Not that there was constantly something to see. A game park was not a zoo, Nicola had said at the start;

animals were not lined up at the roadside waiting to be seen. This was Africa as it had been for centuries. The animals roamed the bush as they had roamed it always.

And yet there was much to see nevertheless. Impala, graceful and dainty, in sun-dappled clearings, while one of the herd, often the biggest, remained alert for danger in the form of a lion or a leopard. There were kudu, regal and beautiful. Once, atop a rise, they came on to a grouping of wildebeeste and zebras, and Nicola explained that the two creatures, the wildebeeste so unkempt, the zebra so majestic, seemed comfortable in each other's company—where one was found you would usually see the other. Zebra were shy animals; Nicola warned that pictures should be shot quickly, before the lovely black and white striped beasts galloped away.

Almost to a person the passengers thrilled to the grey vervet monkeys. Though they would see many more, Blye stopped the bus long enough to let the group enjoy the cheekiness of the little animals with their funny gestures, their boldness in approaching the bus and begging for food—the giving of which was strictly forbidden, Nicola said—and the swinging and gambolling in the branches of the thorn trees. There were baboons too; one old fellow, authoritarian and vicious-looking, was the subject of more than a few photos.

Only Gloria was unenthusiastic. 'You don't care for this?' Derek quizzed her politely, with a wink at Nicola.

Gloria shrugged. 'I'm after bigger game.' She did not look at Derek as she spoke. Her eyes were on Blye, who had turned in his seat and was listening to the comments of the passengers.

Involuntarily Nicola looked at him too. Oddly he was ready for her, his eyes sardonic. Turning away, Nicola said, 'When everyone has finished taking photos I think we could go on.'

'Will we see elephants?' Mrs Barnes wanted to know, pointing to a pile of dung in the road.

'I certainly hope so.' Nicola spoke with a casual friendliness she was far from feeling. 'But that particular mound isn't a clue, Mrs Barnes. Far too ancient. To be interesting it'd have to be new.'

'Have to keep watching for steam,' said Derek, and during the ensuing laughter Nicola forced herself to relax. There were unmistakable undercurrents in this bus, but the enthusiastic reaction of the passengers indicated that they were not bothered by them.

Back at the camp she supervised the preparations for the braaivleis. On succeeding days the tour members would be at liberty to choose their own mode of eating; barbecue stands were provided for those who wished to eat alone, and there was plenty of good frozen meat. But on the first evening there was always a communal braaivleis. This was a Delayney Tours tradition, and one which Nicola thought charming.

By the time the sun began to set all was ready. The camp staff were lighting the fires and the meat was set out on big platters. For a while Nicola was free to relax.

She chose to wander to the fence. The campsite had been carefully chosen, for from this point there was an almost uninterrupted view of the river and the waterhole. The sunset, as colourfully spectacular as any in Africa, was reflected on the water which glowed with tones of scarlet and gold. The sandy river banks were criss-crossed with the footmarks of the many animals which had come to drink at this spot, and at the water's edge three impalas frolicked. Beyond the river lay the bush, vast, brooding, infinitely mysterious in this suspension of time between day and night.

This was the Africa so many people never saw, Nicola reflected. The Africa she had never known herself until recently—exciting, pulsating, primeval.

'Hello, Nicola Sloane, tour-guide,' a familiar voice said.

On the soft ground his footsteps had made no sound. Her pulses quickened, but she kept her head forward, her eyes on the water.

'Hello, Blye,' she countered carefully.

'Enjoy the first day of your new career?'

'Most of it.'

He chuckled, the sound low and disturbingly male on the still air, and she knew the gist of her answer had not escaped him.

'Any tour has its problems,' he said.

'Sure.' A light acknowledgment.

'You have to be able to deal with them.'

'Did I say I couldn't?' For the first time she turned to him and voiced the suspicion that had been in her mind all day. 'I haven't forgotten that I'm on probation. Is that why you're here, Blye? To assess me?'

He laughed again, and she tried to ignore the seductiveness that seemed to reach out to her, almost to touch her.

He would deny it, would say, as he'd said before, that John was ill, that he liked to try new things.

Instead he asked, 'Would you mind?'

Yes! I have to be assessed, I know that. But not by you, Blye Peterson. Especially not by you.

She shrugged. 'One examiner is as good as another, I suppose.'

'Why do you make the word sound synonymous with jailer, I wonder?' On a new note, he said, 'Look, Nicola, an elephant.'

'Where? I don't see. . . .' Despite her training it was hard to believe that there could be anything as large as an elephant where Blye pointed.

And then she saw it—a rounded shape at first, a narrow curving of grey behind the fever trees, the faintest suggestion of movement.

'Incredible!' she breathed. 'I still can't understand that the bush can be so deceptive.'

'It is rather incredible.'

Blye's eyes were on the as yet unseen beast. It was safe to look at him, to marvel at the ruggedness of the profile, the set of lips that was firm yet sensual. To wonder how there could be so much sheer maleness in one man.

A trumpeting call reverberated across the silent land and then the elephant lumbered suddenly through the bush and on to the river bank. It stood on the hoofmarked sand, and for a long moment it did not move. Nicola herself stopped breathing. Silhouetted against the bush, it was magnificent, an awesome memorial to a time long past, when all existing life had been huge.

All at once it flapped its great ears and let out another bellow, and Nicola sucked in her breath. Enraptured, she watched as the elephant made for the river, dipped in its trunk, and then splashed its grey bulk with water.

The group should see this. She was on the point of calling them, of going to knock on each of their bungalows, when something stopped her. There would be other elephants, but there might never be another time quite like this, alone with Blye, sharing with him such a spectacle.

Blye was arrogant. Part of her believed that he had come on this tour to keep an eye on her. Earlier, in his bungalow, he had behaved inexcusably. Yet she knew that she would rather watch this sight with him than without him. She also knew that she would be enjoying it less if there were others around them, exclaiming, clicking cameras. It was a fact she could not deny, though it gave her no joy.

Blye drew out a pipe and began to fill it. She did not need to turn her head to know how he looked—the strong arms and throat, the taut legs, the rugged face that was more eye-catching than all the more conventionally handsome ones she had known.

A woman could love this man. Not Nicola herself, of course. Heavens, not she! She did not even like him very much. But a woman *could* love him, very deeply, and never grow tired of him.

A question trembled on her lips. She had wanted to ask it once before but had suppressed it. Now it came back to her. Until the moment when she actually spoke she was not certain whether she would ask it or not.

'Blye.'

'Yes?'

'Why did you hire me?'

He laughed. 'Now there's a question!'

'Please tell me,' she begged.

'Don't you know?'

'The other applicants were all more qualified than me. That last girl. . . .'

'Had all the experience we were looking for,' he acknowledged reflectively.

'Then why me?'

He had been watching the elephant. Now he turned his head and looked down at her. The setting sun caught his eyes. Whenever she had looked at them she had been caught by their blueness. The blueness of the sea, she thought sometimes, the blueness of the sky. Now they were not blue at all; they were grey, a warmly shimmering colour. She wondered what he was thinking.

'Please Blye, why me?' she asked again.

His look was searching, defying her own eyes to look away, infinitely disturbing.

At last he said, 'A flash of male intuition. I think it was your very nerve in arriving for the interview that appealed to me.'

'Really?' And then, 'Is that all?'

'The other applicants were more experienced, but you had something they lacked.'

'What?' she breathed.

'Enthusiasm. The kind of enthusiasm I haven't seen in a long while. Spirit too.' He was silent a moment before continuing, 'I thought perhaps Delayney Tours had been searching for the wrong qualities.'

Her eyes glowed as she looked at him, and her lips curved in a smile. She was unable to conceal her pleasure from him, and at that moment it didn't seem to matter.

She thought of Morgan's Agricultural, of Mr Morgan's insistence that his staff stay within the limits of his rules. Would the time come when Jonathan would find his father-in-law's rigidity too confining? 'In a way you had quite a nerve of your own,' she said. 'Didn't Delayney Tours mind you stepping out of line?'

He grinned, and for no reason she was reminded of the day in the smart office, the one that had Mr Delayney's name engraved on the door. When she'd asked Blye whether it was all right for him to use the room, his grin had been similar.

She was unprepared for the hand that went to her hair, smoothing a wave of it backward, away from her ear. It was a casual gesture, yet it sent a shock-wave rippling through her.

'We've established that we're both chancers.' That grin again.

'Sure,' she responded unsteadily.

He would remove his hand now that the offending hair was in place, but it remained where it was, the fingers playing softly with the ear-lobe. My goodness, Nicola thought, I've been touched by men many times, Jonathan could be passionate, yet I've never been quite as aware of a man as I am of Blye. I've never been so aware of myself.

The fingers left her ear and trailed to her throat. She could have moved away from him, there was lots of room at the fence, but she didn't.

'You'll make it, Nicola Sloane,' she said softly.

'Oh, I hope so.' The emotion in her voice did not stem from his words of approbation.

'The chance I took will pay off,' said Blye.

'Yes! I'll make you glad that you hired me.'

'Glad?' Blye repeated on an odd note this time. 'I wonder if that's the right word, Nicola.'

His hand had brought them closer. Nicola could sense every inch of the long male body, though she had no actual contact with it. The strange tone of his last words had her head tilting back so that she could see him. His expression was strange too. Her pulses raced even faster than they had before.

He was going to kiss her, right here in the open, where people would see them. She wanted him to. She wanted to feel those sensuous lips on hers. And she knew it was impossible.

'You can't kiss me,' she blurted out.

'Why not? You want me to.' He said it so mockingly that she felt as if she had been struck.

'You're a bastard!' she threw at him, wondering how an atmosphere could change in a matter of seconds.

'The world loves lovers.'

'We don't love each other, Blye Peterson.'

'Just a phrase.' The fingers on her shoulder moved slowly, insolently.

'One I don't care for. And get your fingers off me!'

He took them away. Contradictorily she was disappointed. She was also furious with herself.

At the river the elephant was drinking. It was pouring great sweeps of water from its trunk into its gullet. The honeymooners were watching now, some distance away from Nicola and Blye, binoculars to their eyes. For Nicola the elephant had lost its thrill; it had become an item on the periphery of a mind dominated by Blye—a Blye whom she did not like at all.

'I've things to do,' she announced icily. Without so much as a see-you-at-supper she forced herself to walk away from him.

The African sunset gave way to night. There was not a smidgin of light in the sky by the time the braaivleis got under way. The proceedings were lit by the kerosene lamps that hung from the trees, and by the flickering flashlights held by some of the group.

Later, when the meal had been eaten, a big camp-fire would be lit, but now the smaller fires had been allowed to burn down to the point where there were no flames. From the coals, grey-hot, came a heat that was just right for the piles of steak and chops and boerewors. The smell of cooking meat wafted deliciously through the camp-grounds and the air sizzled with the sound.

Around the fires there was an atmosphere of conviviality. It had been a good day, and people were happy with what they had seen, excited with what might still lie ahead. Nicola moved from one to another, talking, joking, and wondered if anyone could sense the tension that was a hard knot inside her. She was very conscious of Blye's presence, of Gloria, like a second skin beside him wherever he moved. Now and then his eye caught hers, never holding it for long because she deliberately shifted her gaze from his.

But for Blye she would be enjoying this evening. She had spoken the truth at the interview when she had said that she liked people. It was satisfying that through her efforts the tight little groups that commonly exist at the beginning of a tour were beginning to break up, that social barriers were falling. She was glad that Derek was part of the group. He was fun, and the fact that he made no secret of his attraction to her was balm to jarred nerves. It was nice to know that there was a man who accepted her unconditionally.

Soon the meat was ready. The group pronounced everything delicious—the steak, tender and with that special flavour that seems to go with a braai, the spicy boerewors, the chops. The mealies, hot and dripping with butter. There were special compliments for the kebabs, the small pieces of lamb alternating with pieces of green pepper and onion on long thin skewers. Only Gloria withheld comment, but Nicola had not expected praise from her.

By way of dessert there were koeksusters, golden and syrupy. People said they could not manage another bite, yet by the time the meal was over not a koeksuster was left over.

The game-park was in the Lowveld, in the eastern part of southern Africa, where the days are very hot with the sun shafting down in scalding rays. At night it gets very cold. By the time the braaivleis had ended the air was decidedly chilly, so that everyone was glad to gather around the big fire that the camp staff had built. Rugs were brought out and spread on the ground, and there was enough coverage for all to sit. It was a close group, not huddled but cosy, quiet after the meal, content to stare into the leaping flames.

Derek told a tale about whale-hunting in stormy seas. It was a tall story, everyone knew that, but he told it with humour and verve, and by the time he reached the end of it there were others ready to follow with anecdotes of their own.

After a while the story-telling and the jokes petered out. The fire was beginning to burn low when somebody began to strum a guitar. For a few moments, in the dark, Nicola could not see who was playing. Then an ember leapt and she saw it was Blye.

He played softly, slowly, and unbidden

someone came to the fire with logs and started the flames up again. Now Nicola could see Blye's face. In the firelight the ruggedness was not so pronounced. He looked reflective, infinitely human. Nicola wished she could see his eyes.

Beside him was Gloria. She sat so close to him that if she moved any nearer she would be in his lap. Was Gloria one of the women who pursued him for his kisses? Yes, Nicola decided that she was. She wondered what Blye made of the woman's interest in him. Did he mind that she was so obvious?

Deliberately she pushed the questions from her mind, and concentrated instead on the strumming guitar. Something told her that this night, with the camp-fire and the music, was special. Blye might well be arrogant and conceited, his manner overbearing and insufferable, but there was a part of her that was stirred by him—that part was dominant tonight.

Presently he began to sing, and his singing voice was as low and vital as the one he used when he talked. Coming to the end of the song, he started another, a naughty ballad that had his audience laughing. Watching him, listening, Nicola marvelled at a new side to the man, one she had never dreamed existed.

There were songs known and loved by all, and it needed little encouragement for people to join in. As Nicola sang with the others she felt an intense pleasure at a loveliness she would long remember.

Once, just as a song was ending, a roar sounded through the bush. It was an awesome sound, even more so than the elephant's trumpeting had been. Around the camp-fire there was a sudden hush. Another roar, and then another.

'A lion?' Mrs Barnes asked.

Nicola caught Blye's eye across the flames. 'A lion,' she assented. 'Thrilling, isn't it?'

'I'm not sure. . . .' Mrs Barnes was a little frightened. 'It's so nearby!'

It did sound as if the lion was just yards away from them, and perhaps it was. Looking around the group Nicola saw reaction varying from excitement to apprehension. There were those, Derek among them, who would welcome the lion in their midst. Others would be content to see it from the safety of the touring bus.

'It could be miles away,' she said cheerfully. 'Sound carries a long way in the bush at night.'

'But you don't know the lion isn't on the other side of the fence.' This from Gloria.

'I don't,' Nicola agreed. 'I do know that we're in no danger. That lion has no interest in us. It's intent on getting its own supper. Besides, we have our fire, and there are fires at different spots around the fence. It won't come here.'

'Quite a speech,' Gloria commented, and Nicola wondered if she was the only one who heard the malice in the girl's voice.

'Nicola's right.' Blye entered the discussion for the first time. 'We're in no danger at all, Mrs Barnes. How about another song or two before we turn in?'

Softly he began to strum, letting a few bars go by before he started to sing.

> *'Oh, my babby*
> *My curly-headed babby,*
> *I sit beside the fireside*
> *And sing a little song.'*

It was a song Nicola knew from babyhood, one

she had sung with her mother almost before she could form proper sentences. Blye sang alone. None of the others seemed to know the words. After a few moments Nicola added her voice to his.

> 'So lulla-lulla-lulla-bye-bye,
> Do you want the moon to play with,
> Or the stars to run away with,
> They'll come if you don't cry.'

The clear sweet voice of the girl mingled with the low one of the man, echoing through the silence of the African night.

This time when Blye caught her eye across the fire she did not shift her gaze. Within her there was a swell of elation like nothing she had ever known before. They were singing together, for each other. The words belonged to a lullaby, they could have been written for a love-song.

They came to the end of the song, and began again. There were only two people at the fire, Nicola and Blye, quite alone. The others had ceased to exist, as if they had been erased by the darkness and the music. Nicola's voice rose on a tide of sheer exultation. She did not take her eyes from Blye. She did not see Gloria beside him, was unaware of Derek beside herself.

The singing ended and there was a burst of applause. Looking around her, at the smiling faces, Nicola felt as if she had come quite suddenly upon an unexpected crowd of people. She felt a sense of shock, and wondered how she could have lost her sense of reality so completely.

The magic—surely there had been magic for a few minutes—did not last long. In an odd tone Derek commented, 'That was very nice,' and a moment later Gloria, 'How about some adult music now, Blye?'

'Just one more song. Nicola has plans for an early start tomorrow I believe,' Blye said easily.

'That's right,' Nicola agreed in her most down-to-earth manner. 'We leave camp at sunrise.'

Blye was looking at her again. It was too dark to see his eyes, but she did not need to. She could sense that they were sardonic. Had the lovely song meant nothing to him? He could not have missed her own emotion. Perhaps, like Gloria, he had been amused by it.

Gloria had her hand on his arm. She was sitting even closer to him than before. On her face was an expression that Nicola recognised—dislike mixed with gloating. You sang with him, she seemed to be saying. I'll do a lot more with him than that. Soon, when the rest of you are in bed. And what we do then will be entirely adult.

Nicola felt her cheeks flame.

Blye, she saw, made no effort to dislodge Gloria's hand. She felt Derek put an arm around her shoulder. Her inclination was to withdraw, then she saw Blye's lips tighten. So he had not missed the gesture. Lifting her chin, she smiled across at him.

Something had happened to her while they were singing. She had let a mood, an emotion, get the better of her. It had to do with a lullaby that was part of the fabric of her childhood. Even more it had to do with Blye.

He could stir her, he could arouse in her emotions of anger and of joy. But only because she let him. Choice was involved, she told herself fiercely. Her own choice.

Jonathan had wrought havoc in her life. She

had let him do it—she knew that now. True, they had been engaged, but she should have seen the signs, should have understood him well enough to know that he was influenced by money, by position, should have realised that when Mr Morgan's daughter arrived in town, single, pretty, undeniably eligible, Jonathan would be tempted. Maggie had known. Wise Maggie! Had Nicola listened to her, she would not have been quite so shattered when Jonathan ended the engagement.

She could not dwell on Jonathan and what had been. To do so would be to ruin her life. But she could profit from the experience. With her erstwhile fiancé there had at least been love of a kind. With Blye there was nothing, not even affection. He was not her type of man, and never could be.

It did not matter a damn whether he spent the night alone or with Gloria. Nicola did not care, would not *let* herself care.

Thank heavens for Derek. He would be her friend for the duration of this tour. Lighthearted, never serious for long, Derek meant nothing by his flirtatiousness. It was just that, and that was how she wanted it.

Derek's hand tightened fractionally and she did not withdraw. She let her head lean on his shoulder, and grinned again at a grim-faced Blye, provocatively this time.

CHAPTER FOUR

DESPITE a night that was not entirely restful, Nicola was up long before daybreak. She wanted to be dressed and ready before it was time to knock on doors. On leaving the camp-fire last night she'd requested that the group be ready by five-thirty. There had been grumbles—'A holiday and our guide won't let us sleep!'—but they had been goodnatured. Everyone understood that the early dawn was the best time to see animals. Even Gloria seemed to know the procedure—unless she just did not want to be left behind where she could not see Blye, Nicola mused uncharitably.

Intentions would be good, the instructor had warned at the training session, but there were always some who overslept. A tour-guide should make sure her group was awake—no matter how much people professed to enjoy their sleep, they were inevitably upset if they missed something exciting.

The ground was wet underfoot as she walked from one bungalow to the next. Bushes and shrubs were webbed with dew, and the air was cold. 'Be sure to dress warmly,' Nicola called at each door, and was glad of her own thick sweater. After an hour or two they would return to camp for breakfast. It would be hot by then, and everyone would have a chance to change into summer clothes. She had told them that also.

She glanced at her watch, and saw that she had some time to kill. She could go back to her bungalow and lie on her bed, close her eyes and catch up on some of the sleep she had missed. Or she could take a walk through the camp-grounds and enjoy the early morning on her own. She opted for the latter, and as she breathed in air that was like chilled champagne she was glad of the choice.

In half an hour it would be light enough to see. Derek had wanted to leave even earlier, but there were rules about driving in the dark. On unlit roads it was almost impossible to see animals, all too easy to run them over.

It was still dark now, but as Nicola stood by the fence and looked in the direction of the waterhole she could make out shapes. Bushes or animals? Bushes perhaps, but it was fun to speculate.

She savoured the stillness—the utter stillness of the veld. No zooming of cars or clanging of bicycles, no buzz of voices, of shouting and argument.

It was still, but not quiet, for the veld had a voice of its own. Thre was the sound of the crickets, muted now that dawn was here. There was the sound of the breeze ruffling the long grass. And there were the sounds that were unique to a game park, high-pitched cries and shufflings in the bush, invisible testimony that there were animals out there. A high barking echoed against the distant kopjes. Not the barking of a dog, for there were no dogs here. Baboons, and not all that far away, Nicola thought.

'Up early,' someone said, and she knew she'd heard the voice in her dreams last night.

She put a hand to the fence, as if she needed to

steady herself. 'Killing time,' she responded lightly.

'I think it's more than that,' said Blye. 'You could have napped a while longer. You love this place, Nicola.'

A fact, not a question. He was so sure of himself at all times—sure in a way that Jonathan had not been. Jonathan had thought he knew what he wanted, and all the time he had wanted something very different.

'Yes,' she said, 'I love it. You're up early too, Blye.'

'It seems we have something else in common.' He smiled down at her.

Her heart beat suddenly faster. 'Both drawn to the veld, you mean.'

'I never tire of it.'

'You could drive a bus permanently,' she teased.

He chuckled. In the dark stillness the sound was unnerving. 'I've brought you some coffee.'

He had evaded the question. Not that it needed answering. Blye was a man whose place was in a big corporation. And not in a personnel office, Nicola thought, but in a place where bigger decisions were made. His air of power and authority were an integral part of him. He could as soon shed these qualities as he could rid himself of his virile masculinity. He was a man who would be obeyed by others, who would be looked up to by them. It was hard to believe that he did not have a position of more importance in the offices of Delayney Tours.

She looked at him as he handed her a cup. His sweater was a casual garment that reached to his chin, yet she felt as if she could see through the wool to the superb body, to the muscled tautness that would be with Blye even as he was asleep.

Dim as it was, she could make out his face, the eyes beneath their thick brows, the rugged cheekbones, the hard sweep of jaw. The curve of smiling lips. Not for the first time she wondered how it would feel to be kissed by him.

Quite involuntarily she took a step closer to him—and stopped. She dropped her eyes, appalled. Last night she had made a decision not to think about Blye, not to let herself respond to him. It was a decision she meant to keep.

'I have to go,' she said, a little unsteadily.

'Your little bunch is still more asleep than awake.' He spoke gently—as if, Nicola thought even more appalled, he knew how she felt.

'A couple of things that need doing,' she murmured.

'They're all done. Drink your coffee, Nicola.'

He was right, of course. She had seen to all her preparations last night. In the circumstances, to refuse the coffee was childish. Blye Peterson must never think of her as a child.

Besides, this was what she wanted, to stand here with him, drinking coffee in the half-light. She wanted to stand close to him, with his arm brushing hers, sharing the mystic bushveld dawn. Logic and decisions notwithstanding.

The coffee was hot and strong, and she drank just a few sips at a time, wanting to savour it. Leaning her arms on the fence, she held the cup in front of her. Steam from the coffee rose in the cold air. It merged with the steam from Blye's cup. As their voices had merged last night. Nicola wondered whether the analogy had occurred to him.

'Look.' He pointed.

A duiker stood a yard or two from the camp fence. The graceful body of the deer was poised and alert, ears and tail quivering. Its eyes were on the two humans, wary and yet curious.

'It's not even scared of us,' Nicola observed in wonder.

'It knows whom it can trust.'

'How?'

'Instinct.' He paused, and when he spoke again his voice has hardened. 'Are you as sure of your own feelings, Nicola?'

Did he know that he had caught her on the raw? 'I hope so,' she said carefully.

'I wonder.'

'What are you getting at?'

'I was thinking,' he said smoothly, 'of Derek. And of the man you left behind.'

The breath skittered in her chest. The hand that held the cup had to grip tightly, otherwise the coffee would have spilled.

'I didn't tell you about Jonathan!' she gasped.

'So his name was Jonathan.'

He had baited a trap and she had fallen into it, without a struggle. The duiker would have done better, she thought in disgust.

'I didn't tell you about him,' she said again.

'You didn't have to.'

She took a moment to digest the statement, then she turned on him hotly. 'You had me checked!'

'You know better than that. No, Nicola, on your ring finger there was a fading mark, and your eyes were unhappy.'

She remembered the interview. You're married? About to be married? She'd answered no to both questions. He had not questioned her further, but all the time he had known there was a Jonathan.

'Divorced?' Blye asked now.

Do you have to know? Why didn't you ask at the time if you were so interested? And why, oh, why are you so damned perceptive?

She took a shuddering breath. 'Jilted. An old-fashioned word.'

'Ugly too.'

Nicola took a sip from her coffee, and wished he'd spiked it with brandy. At this moment she could have done with the support it was rumoured to give.

'Ugly,' she agreed.

'Want to talk about it?'

Nicola shrugged. Her eyes were on the steam of the two coffees, but the wonder had gone out of the sight. Blye Peterson wanted to know the facts about the girl he had hired. She had been crazy to endow the mingling steam with a magic and a meaning it did not possess.

'It's not an unusual story. We worked in the same firm, fell in love—or thought we did—and got engaged. Then the daughter of the boss arrived on the scene.' Her voice was at variance with the clipped nature of her words.

'What a fool he must have been. You're well rid of him.' Blye's tone was hard. Before Nicola could make anything of the statement, he went on, 'Do you still love him?'

I thought I did. Now I wonder if I ever loved him at all—really loved him. I find myself thinking more about you, Blye Peterson, than I do about Jonathan.

'No,' she said truthfully.

Blye took her hand. His fingers were long and cool, firm and strong. Like the rest of him.

'It still hurts?'

Nicola hesitated before saying, 'A little.'

The fingers began a slow stroking, causing the blood to race in her veins. 'Rejection does hurt.'

And who has hurt you? You look so unvulnerable, as if the woman in any relationship would be the one to be hurt. Was there a woman who let you down? It would account for your attitude towards all women.

'Jonathan is the reason you applied for the job.'

Another statement. The arrogance of the man, to assume that he knew her thoughts, her motives!

Nicola looked him straight in the eye. 'No. It's what I always dreamed of.'

'So the timing was coincidental?'

'Not entirely. It's true that I was unhappy, that I wanted to get away. It's also true that from the first time I travelled with my parents I wanted to be a tour-guide myself.'

'I see.'

'Do you?' Your turn to be interrogated, Mr Blye Peterson. 'Why do you want to know so much?' she asked. 'Sorry you gave me the job?'

'No.'

'Feel you should have been more persistent in your questioning? Do Delayney Tours need to know every personal detail of their employees' lives? Do you want to know how many times I brush my hair at night and which shoe I take off first? Do you want to know. . . .'

He cut in. 'Stop it, Nicola! Jeering doesn't suit you.'

In her anger she had not noticed that his hand

was still on hers. He had put his coffee-cup in the other hand and the steam no longer mingled. She tried to move away and found that his grip was surprisingly firm.

'What *do* you want?' she asked.

'Many things. Can you guess at them, Nicola?'

His voice was soft, so infinitely seductive that she found herself trembling. 'Time we got going,' she said unsteadily.

'You're a tour-guide, my dear. Are you also a woman?'

'Of course I'm a woman!'

'I'm glad.' His eyes were disturbingly enig-matic.

He turned to her, took the cup from her and put it with his own on the ground. Cupping her face with his hands, the tips of his fingers resting just below her hairline, he looked down at her. His eyes were no colour at all yet, but she could see the intensity of his gaze. Her trembling increased.

'Blye, the time!' she exclaimed.

'It's early, are you so scared of me, Nicola?'

'I'm not scared at all!'

'And that, I think, could be another lie.' The thumbs moved, stroking her cheeks.

To cover a sudden giddiness, Nicola said, 'I'm not scared, heavens, why should I be? I'm twenty-one, Blye, people will be coming now.'

'You're talking too much. I want you to be careful of Derek.'

'Derek?' The name burst out in astonishment.

'It hasn't escaped you that he likes you. There's a Derek on every tour. They tend to think the guide is thrown in as part of the amusement.'

'How dare you!'

'And when the tour is over they vanish. A novice guide is likely to be left with a broken heart.'

'So you're warning me.'

Blye was still stroking her cheeks. Slowly, rhythmically, with a poignance that stirred her senses to a frenzy. If only he would stop! *Did* she want him to stop?

'You could call it a warning. You've had one bad experience. Derek could be dangerous for you.'

Derek is just a very nice man who's helped me over a few difficult moments. If anyone is dangerous that person is you, Blye Peterson. I try to tell myself otherwise, yet I know it's not true.

The flash of insight shocked her—shook her. Involuntarily she looked up at him. He was a perceptive man, already he knew too much about her. It would not do to have him read her thoughts now.

It was this thought that drove her to say bitingly, 'Derek dangerous? Heavens, Blye, men like Derek have been in and out of my life. If anything, he should be scared of me.'

'I don't believe you.' His voice was harsh, and his fingers pressed into the soft skin, hurting her.

'It's true. Jonathan just happened to be one of them. I was hurt by his rejection—any woman would have been. That's all there was to it.'

'Stop this!' he grated.

'I haven't finished. You asked me if I was a woman. I have been for a long time.'

And what will you say to that? Tell me again you don't believe me?

His answer was not long in coming. 'Prove it.'

'What?'

'I said prove it. Come to bed with me.'

A little desperately Nicola looked around her. Words were so easy to say. If only their consequences were as easy to live with! 'The time,' she remembered.

'I don't mean now, honey. Tonight.'

'Your room or mine?' she taunted, knowing no other way to cope with a situation that was entirely of her own making.

'Yours.' His hands dropped from her face.

'Fine.' It was hard to get the word out casually. Tonight it would be harder still to find a way out. But find one she would. She had never slept with a man yet, and she was not about to begin now, with a man who could mean nothing to her.

'Fine, is it? Let me give you a brief appetiser.'

The words should have warned her, but the tone was so mild that as his arms closed around her she was caught unprepared. There was no escaping Blye as his lips found her mouth. The breath seemed to have been jerked from her lungs, so that for a moment she lay limply against him.

The pressure of his lips increased, and adrenalin flooded her system. How dared he treat her like this! True, she had wondered sometimes how it would feel to be kissed by him—but this, this total assumption that he could kiss her because that was his choice, was outrageous. She struggled against him.

In vain. The arms holding her tightened as the kiss became more demanding, forcing her lips apart, coaxing a response from her.

She gasped in shock as hands, chilled by the cool air, slid beneath her sweater on to warm bare skin. Sensuously they moved on her back, shaping themselves to her shoulders, and then downward, slowly, to her waist. As Nicola's excitement mounted, her shock faded. Outrage faded too as a kiss that had begun with force became a mutually satisfying experience.

Blye's sweater was rough against her throat, and she could feel his legs, taut and hard against hers. Swept with a sudden longing, she was about to put her arms around his neck.

Blye chose that moment to break the embrace. He pushed her a little away from him, and she stared up at him, dazed.

'Not bad,' he commented.

Nicola found her voice. 'You're looking for perfection?'

'Why not?' His voice was dry. 'You'll have another chance at it tonight, Nicola.'

'You're an utter swine!' she flung at him.

'I'm also an excellent lover. Don't bother to parry that one, honey. In case you're wondering why we stopped—I heard a door open.'

Saved by the group. Had she wanted to be saved? Seconds earlier the answer might have been no, but now she was glad. Her head was spinning and her legs felt as weak as if they had been severed from her body. Nevertheless she managed to say, with a coolness she was far from feeling, 'We'd have stopped anyway. I'd had enough.'

Blye did not answer. He did not need to. The husky laugh was sufficient evidence that he did not believe her. Nicola put a hand to cheeks that should have been cool and found they were burning.

She made to turn away when Blye put a hand on her arm. 'About Derek. Remember that. . . .'

What she was to remember was never articulated, for just then someone called, 'Blye? Blye, is that you?' and seconds later Gloria materialised through the trees. She stopped short when she saw Nicola and Blye so close together, and for a moment her face was far from pleasant. She recovered herself quickly. In honeyed tones she said, 'What a glorious morning! And what an early start you both must have made.'

'You're early yourself.' Blye was smiling down at her. In his voice Nicola heard none of the mockery that was too often directed at herself.

There was nothing in his manner to show that he had just experienced a love scene. What had left Nicola feeling shattered had clearly meant nothing to Blye.

Without a word she turned on her heel and walked away. She doubted whether the other two, now embarked on a lively conversation, even knew she had gone.

Nicola did not go straight to the bus. Instead she went to her room where the mirror reflected dishevelled hair and wild eyes. It was galling to realise that Blye and Gloria had seen her in this state!

Fiercely she splashed cold water on to her face, then brushed her hair with quick hard strokes. She did not want to see Blye and Gloria, not so soon, but she had no option. The group was waiting to leave. She could not be late. Glancing at her watch, she saw she had a minute to spare— incredible that so much could have happened in so short a time—and when she reached the bus she found she was the last to arrive.

Almost immediately she was aware that

something was wrong. Some silences are companionable and relaxed, the one she encountered now was anything but that. It was a silence fraught with tension and hostility. It was a few seconds before Nicola saw the cause. When she did she was very angry.

In the front seat, the one where yesterday Mrs Barnes had been, Gloria was now sitting. Mrs Barnes was at the back of the bus. She looked uncomfortable and upset. The other passengers seemed tense. Only Gloria was unperturbed. The brilliant smile she gave to Nicola was a challenge.

Nicola turned to Blye. As he met her eyes she saw that his own were more impassive than she had seen them. Gloria might be a special friend, it was nevertheless up to Nicola to deal with her.

'With our guide finally arrived there's nothing to hold us up, I believe,' Gloria said in a husky voice which Nicola supposed some might consider sexy.

With an effort she concealed her fury. Pleasantly she said, 'We'll leave when you have changed places with Mrs Barnes.'

'I have no intention of changing.'

'We'll wait until you do.' Politely.

She saw rather than heard the group expel their breath, and she knew they were on the side of the elderly lady. They want me to stand my ground, Nicola thought.

'I got here first,' said Gloria.

'It makes no difference. I did explain yesterday that it's our policy that passengers retain their seats throughout the tour.'

'Get going, Gloria!' Derek called, only to be rewarded with a chilling look from the lady in question. He meant well, Nicola knew, but she wished he had remained silent.

'Blye,' Gloria appealed, 'why don't you say something?'

'Leave our driver out of this, please,' Nicola ordered, quickly, before Blye could speak. Would he have spoken? 'I'm in control here.'

'You know as well as I do that Blye is not just a driver.'

Over the ripple of sound in the bus—damn the woman and her venomous manner!—Nicola countered firmly, 'That is his capacity on this tour. I'm asking you for the last time to change places with Mrs Barnes.'

'If I don't?'

'We'll spend the day in camp.'

Gloria did not react right away. Her face had gone very pale, only on the high cheekbones two brilliant spots of red burned. Looking down, Nicola saw that her own knuckles were white and tight on the clip-board. Behind her Blye sat motionless; it was so quiet on the bus that had he moved so much as a fingertip she would have heard him. She could not see him, but she could not have been more aware of him than she was at this moment.

'For heaven's sake!' Derek exclaimed, and then Jim Slade said, 'Get your act together, Mrs Payne. You're spoiling things for us all.'

In a smooth snakelike movement Gloria got to her feet. The look she shot Nicola was snakelike too. The next moment Nicola felt a vicious kick on one of her shins. Somehow she stifled a gasp and looked down quickly to hide the tears of pain which gathered in her eyes. By the time she had regained her composure Gloria was seated at the back of the bus and Mrs Barnes was making her way up the aisle.

Turning to Blye, Nicola said, 'We can go now.' Would he say something? she wondered. Had he seen the kick? And she knew that he hadn't. Nobody had seen it, Gloria's cleverness had taken care of that.

He did not speak, and his face was still without expression. But in his eyes something flickered. Approval for the way she had handled the situation? It should mean nothing to her, Nicola knew, but as she turned back to the group she felt proud of herself.

As Blye started the bus and drove out of the camp gates the passengers turned their faces to the windows. With the incident ended it seemed their minds were now on the awakening bushveld. But Gloria had not forgotten, Nicola knew, and Blye was a man who would forget very little. As for Nicola herself, as her eyes searched the veld for movement she could not help wondering what other problems lay ahead.

There was general agreement among the passengers that it had been worth while getting up early, otherwise they might never have known the haunting quality of the veld at dawn—the mist that hovered over the river, the silhouetted shapes of trees and bushes, the brooding sky.

Most exciting, naturally, was the wild life. The bus was not far out of camp when a warthog came out of the bush and ambled comically across the road. It was too dark for photos, but it was worth stopping all the same. Blye was about to go on when Nicola spotted more movement. 'Wait,' she told him, and was gratified when three more of the tusky creatures appeared.

Here and there along the way were monkeys. Always spirited, in the early morning they had an added verve that brought many laughs from the group. Blye stopped the bus alongside one volatile family. Within seconds monkeys had leaped to the windows and were making cheeky gestures as they begged in vain for food. Mrs Barnes laughed so much that she had to wipe the tears from her eyes. 'I never get tired of the little rascals,' she said to Nicola. 'I wish I could take one home as a pet.'

'And wouldn't you be getting more than you bargain for!' Nicola told her, smiling. Looking at the elderly lady, her painful leg stretched out in the space the front seat provided, she knew that Mrs Barnes's comfort was justification in itself for the stand she had taken against Gloria.

The monkeys were everywhere now. They clung to the widows, to the radiator; they made thudding noises as they played on the roof of the bus. The more they frolicked the more the watching humans delighted. Nicola would have liked to let them enjoy themselves a while longer but it was time to go on and she signalled to Blye. As the bus started, most of the monkeys jumped to the road, but two remained, clinging determinedly to the beading around the windows. Half a mile on first one jumped into the road, and then the other. Spontaneously the passengers clapped.

The group had forgotten the earlier tension, and it was time she did too, Nicola decided. Picking up her microphone, she announced that they were headed for the river.

'This is drinking time?' Jim Slade wanted to know.

'Nearing the end of it. Many animals go to the river, while it's still dark, but of course we can't drive then.' She smiled, 'Let's hope there'll still be enough for us to see.'

There was an almost unimpeded view of the waterhole. A collective gasp came from the passengers as Blye drew up beside a clump of maroela trees. On the sandy bank below them were more animals than they had yet seen.

Nicola turned to Blye. 'It's like a picture from a safari brochure!'

'It really is special,' he agreed, and there was something in his voice that made her wonder whether it was a love of animals that had prompted him to volunteer to drive when John had been taken ill.

Two huge herds, one of zebra, the other of wildebeeste, were spread over the bank. A few kudus had finished drinking and were leaving the river. Not far from them were sable antelope. Impalas were everywhere, and at the river's edge three giraffes straddled long legs so that their necks could reach the water.

Nicola and Blye saw the elephant at the same moment. As yet it was the merest suggestion of movement, a waving curve of grey ear above a mass of trees, but that it was an elephant, Nicola did not doubt. The passengers buzzed with excitement when she told them. They pressed their faces to the windows, staring in the direction of Nicola's pointing hand. And then, quite suddenly, there it was, an enormous elephant, ears flapping, trunk waving. It stopped at the edge of the bush and wrapped its trunk around a slender tree. In seconds the tree had snapped.

'As I would break a match!' Jim Slade commented, awed.

Presently it made for the river and sank its trunk in the water. Over the exclamations of the group, Blye said, 'Recognise him, Nicola?'

'The one we saw last night?'

'Sure of it. That's our old fellow.'

Perhaps it was, and perhaps it wasn't. Nicola did not care. What mattered was a quite absurd happiness at the word 'our', at the shared experience.

She turned and looked at him. He was smiling, a wonderful smile that extended to his eyes, with no hint of the hateful mockery in it. She took a step towards him, then stopped. Even with no people around them she could not give in to her impulse to touch his hair and the lines around his mouth. She did not have the right. Probably she never would.

'You did well.' He spoke very quietly.

'Spotting the elephant? You saw it too, Blye.'

'Handling Gloria.' Blye's voice was pitched low so that only Nicola could hear him.

Warmed, she said, 'I had to do it.'

'Right. But go carefully, Nicola.'

'In what way?'

'You don't like her.'

'Have I said that?'

'It shows.'

Nicola was quiet a moment. Then she said, 'It's not an easy situation.'

'She's a customer, Nicola.'

What else is she? A woman to whom you're attracted? Certainly one who makes no bones about liking you.'

'Nicola?'

Tone subdued, she said, 'I'll be careful.'

CHAPTER FIVE

BREAKFAST was a cheerful affair. The sun was quite high in the sky and already there was the promise of heat. The meal over, people went to their bungalows to change into summer clothes. Nicola thought Mrs Barnes looked a little pale, but when she suggested that the elderly woman might like to stay in camp for the morning she protested. Mrs Barnes had come to see animals, and she would see them.

See them she did, for the morning was a great success—more elephants, a herd of water buffalo, dangerous beasts with curving horns and lethal temperaments. Hundreds of impala and monkeys.

Most memorable of all was the leopard. A rare sighting indeed, for the sleek animal is shy and seldom seen. Nicola saw it first and the excitement of watching it run, fast as an arrow through the dun-coloured bush, restored a spirit that had been low since her talk with Blye.

After lunch, and back at the camp, Derek was exuberant. 'You gave us all a thrill with that leopard, Nicola!' he declared.

'You make it sound as if I was responsible for its being there!'

'You spotted it.'

Nicola burst out laughing. 'Good pun, Derek— I like that!'

'And I like you.' They were standing together by the fence, looking out over the river, and now an arm went around her shoulders. 'You're a fantastic guide, Nicola.'

'Thank you, kind sir.'

'And a fantastic girl.'

'And you're irrepressible!' She smiled up at him, wondering why she could be so relaxed with one man when with another she was tight as a coiled spring.

'Why not just call me sexy?' His eyes sparkled with mischief. 'Women fall over themselves to get near me, did you know?'

The man women probably did fall over themselves to be near was Blye. She was not going to think about Blye! 'I know one woman who doesn't,' she grinned. 'I don't think Gloria falls for you.'

'She's too preoccupied with our driver.'

After a moment Nicola said, 'Perhaps she is.'

'Conceited bitch! We should have thrown Gloria Payne out as food for the leopard. Now why didn't I think of it?'

'Why didn't I?' Nicola wiped laughter tears from her eyes.

'Miss Sloane,' said a dangerous voice.

Nicola felt her heart give a thud as her head jerked up. 'Blye,' she responded unsteadily as she looked into a pair of ice-blue eyes.

'I want to talk to you,' he said.

'Not now,' Derek protested. 'Nicola and I were just enjoying a joke.'

'At the expense of a member of our group.'

'Who asked for it,' Derek defended.

'Come with me, please.' Ignoring Derek, Blye spoke frostily to Nicola.

'Don't play the heavy boss with her, Peterson.' Derek was flushed and frowning. Tense as she was, Nicola could not help noticing that he looked very young beside Blye, a little unsure of himself. And she wondered why she was making comparisons.

'Nicola,' Blye ordered.

'You're only the driver. Leave her alone.'

'Derek, please.' Nicola put a cautionary hand on his. 'In a way Blye does have authority.'

'But. . . .'

'I'll see you later.'

Her tone was far from conciliatory when she turned on Blye a few minutes later. 'How dare you treat me like this!' she flung at him.

'I merely asked you to come with me.'

'Very rudely.'

'I thought I was being extremely polite—in the circumstances,' said Blye.

'It's that icy tone that makes it rude, and that arrogant expression of yours.' She stopped short. 'What do you mean by the circumstances? I did nothing wrong.' She bit her lip. 'Except that I talked about Gloria.'

'In a very derogatory way.'

'It was a joke,' Nicola was defensive.

'Was it?' Blye drawled.

Nicola decided to capitulate. 'All right then, I'd love to throw her to a leopard, but the joke was in bad taste, for which I'm sorry. No harm done, Blye, she was nowhere near us.'

'May I remind you once again that Gloria Payne is a paying guest of this safari. If you've something to say about her come to me. You have no right to discuss one member of the group with another.'

'You really are doing the heavy boss act!' Nicola mocked.

There was the merest flicker of blue eyes before Blye went on. 'Which brings me to another point. Delayney Tours doesn't permit fraternisation between passengers and staff.'

'You didn't seem to mind when I sat with Mrs Barnes before lunch. I thought friendliness was a desirable quality in a guide.

'Friendliness is one thing. Pairing off is another.'

She stared at him. 'I haven't paired off with Derek!'

'You let him put his arm around you.'

'There was nothing to it. For heaven's sake, Blye, even you can't see an ulterior motive behind every friendly gesture!'

In the gaunt face the lips were set, the expression bleak. There was something un-yielding in the long strong line of the jaw. No wonder Derek had looked young and unsure of himself beside Blye. It would take a remarkable man to match him.

'It's not to happen again,' was all he said.

He *was* playing the heavy boss. True, this was Nicola's first safari. True too that as the person who had hired her Blye had some authority over her. But he did not have the right to be so autocratic.

He was turning to go when Nicola said, 'You couldn't be jealous?'

In a second he had spun on his heel, the movement bringing him closer to her. He looked very tall, very powerful—dangerous.

'Jealous?' He was grinning, his teeth white and wicked against his tan. Nicola felt her pulses racing.

Keep cool, she thought. Don't let him see how he affects me. Aloud she asked, 'Why not?'

His hands went to her shoulders, cupping them. On legs that were like water she tried to step away from him, to the side of him, and found she could not move.

'Derek is a child,' he said. 'I don't waste my energy being jealous of children.'

He was so close to her that she felt dizzy. His open-necked shirt formed a vee, and her eyes, on a level with his throat, could see the strong thrust of it, as well as the hair that curled at the top of his chest.

The sight brought back the memory of his kisses. She was filled with a sudden and irrational longing to have him kiss her again, and she had to make a conscious effort not to move towards him. Let Blye know the extent of his power over her and he would become even more impossible than he had been until now.

With an effort she kept her mind on the conversation. 'Derek isn't a child.'

'By my definition he is. Not that it matters.' His tone had lost its coolness. It was soft now, seductive, fire to frenzied nerves.

'Why not?' she whispered.

He laughed. 'Because we have an arrangement, Nicola.'

She could not speak, and he laughed again. A hand went to her chin, tilting her head, forcing her to look at him. 'Your bungalow—tonight. You couldn't have forgotten?'

Would any woman forget? It was becoming increasingly hard to breathe. Somehow Nicola managed to smile. 'There are things I don't forget.'

'Ah.' The eyes that studied her were very blue, their expression unreadable as they lingered on a small face that had suddenly gone very pale, on lips that trembled, on the pulse that beat too quickly at the base of a vulnerable throat.

'And you haven't changed your mind?'

Later it occurred to her that she could have said, 'Yes—yes, I have changed my mind, your behaviour was unpardonable, and it's not something I can overlook.' Righteous indignation would have given her the excuse she needed. But hindsight is always easy. At this particular moment Nicola knew only that to say she had changed her mind would make her seem a child too, a being less than Gloria.

She gave what she hoped was an indifferent shrug. 'Of course not.'

The expression, whatever it signified, deepened. 'Then we agree,' Blye said, even more softly, 'that I have no reason to be jealous of Derek.'

The afternoon excursion was exciting—more animals, more lovely sights. Nicola enjoyed none of it. Mechanically she performed her functions, a robot that smiled and talked and responded on cue. Nobody noticed. Almost nobody. Now and then a pair of blue eyes rested on her face, narrowed, enigmatic, and then she would force herself to behave with heightened vivacity.

Even Blye, she felt sure, could not guess at the turmoil raging inside her. Perhaps he still wondered if she had second thoughts about the night to come. But he could not know the extent of her fear. She had given him to understand that she was experienced in the ways of men, the last thing he would expect was a virgin.

Oh yes, she was frightened—frightened in a

way that was strange, for she was also conscious of a wild longing. It was a feeling she had never experienced before, not with Jonathan, not with other men before him. It was something she had felt for the first time in Blye's arms.

The afternoon wore on and the turmoil did not resolve itself. Easy enough just to tell Blye that she had in fact changed her mind. Yet not easy at all. Blye would know her for the coward she was. At best he'd be amused, at worst he would be openly contemptuous.

Yet what chance did she have? Notwithstanding the fact that many women would leap at the chance to have Blye make love to them, Nicola knew that she herself had no choice at all. She wanted him, yes—no point in denying it to herself. It was a wanting that gnawed inside her, an agonising sensation that owed nothing to logic, that would not be pushed away however hard she tried. The most confusing sensation—painful yet spine-tinglingly delicious at the same time. But she also had principles that were inbred and strong—she could not abandon them.

When would Blye come to her? Late. When the fire had died and the members of the group were alseep. She would open her door, and she would tell him that she did not feel well. He would give the mocking grin that so infuriated her, would suggest that he did not believe her, and she would tell him, very firmly, that it was his privilege to believe what he wished. And then she would close the door.

Objective achieved. How she would face him in the morning was another matter.

Afternoon turned to evening. The fires were lit and soon the aroma of roasting meat wafted through the night air. Nicola moved from one member of the group to another, laughing, talking, vivacious. All the time she was aware of Blye. Even when she did not see him she could have pinpointed his position. It was as if he was possessed of a special magnetism, one that reached out to her, drawing her into the web of an intoxicating masculinity. She did not need to see him to know where he was; in fact she made a deliberate effort not to look his way.

It was not possible to avoid him completely. Once, feeling she was being watched, she looked up without thought as to who the other person might be. Blye's gaze met hers, and even in the dark she could see that it was sardonic. Though he was a little distance away from her, she was as aware of him as if he had been beside her, the long lithe body touching hers. For a long moment she could not shift her eyes from his. And then she saw one eyelid descend in a wink that was as deliberate as it was outrageous. As Nicola turned away she felt her heart thud against her rib-cage.

If the braaivleis was a success—to judge by the excess of good humour around the fire it must have been—then Nicola did not know it. She was conscious only of the tall figure, sinuously attractive in the flickering light, and of a mouth that was becoming more dry by the minute. Gloria was never far from Blye. She seemed stuck to his side, as if glued to him, Nicola thought viciously. She wonderd what Gloria would say if she knew of the planned rendezvous. On the heels of the thought came another. Perhaps Gloria need say nothing, perhaps Blye had changed his mind, had decided that the woman's voluptuous charms were more inviting than anything Nicola had to offer. Perhaps he would find Gloria's bungalow more appealing after all. It was a thought that should have brought relief, but oddly it made for pain.

As the fire died people began to say their goodnights. Nicola was the last to leave the fire. The camp staff would clean up, but she found things to keep her busy a while longer. Only when Blye had been gone some time did she make her way to her bungalow.

She opened the door and switched on the light, then gasped. A man lay on the bed, one long leg crossed over the other, eyes closed.

'Blye!' she exclaimed.

One eye opened, the eye that had winked at her so outrageously just an hour earlier.

'What are you doing here?'

Lazily he raised himself. With the catlike grace of a jungle animal he got off the bed. Then he said, very mildly, 'I thought you knew the answer to that.'

He was wearing dark trousers and a matching turtlenecked sweater, the clothes sleekly well fitting on the superb figure. He looked taller than ever, infinitely more dangerous. There was something primeval about him, Nicola thought. She had noticed it in the offices of Delayney Tours when he had interviewed her. In the dimly-lit bungalow far from civilisation the quality was emphasised.

She wetted dry lips and said the first thing that came to mind. 'I didn't think you'd come.'

'No?' Could a voice be mocking and seductive at the same time? 'We had an arrangement.'

'Right. Right we had.'

Think! Think quickly. How do I get out of this?

'Well then?' softly.

Nicola tossed her head. 'We had an argument after that. I'd have thought it changed the situation.'

'What I think,' Blye pronounced silkily, 'is that you're scared.'

'Scared!' The word bounced out unsteadily. 'Why on earth should I be scared?'

'You tell me.' His eyes held hers, and she thought they looked amused. Then they slid downwards, over the curved feminine body. 'You're an experienced woman, Nicola, and experienced women aren't scared of a little fun.'

Fun? Is that all it means to you, Blye? How you'd laugh if you knew that my whole being is in a state of shock!

'I am experienced,' she said as firmly as she could. 'And I'm not scared. Not of you, Blye.'

'Good. Come here, Nicola.'

Just like that. The awful thing was that she wanted to go to him. Despite the nervousness fluttering inside her she wanted to go to him.

She shook her head. 'Not tonight.'

He took a step closer towards her. His presence was overpowering in the small room, all-encompassing. The air crackled with ten-sion—a sexual tension, Nicola realised, and knew she had never encountered anything quite like it before.

She stepped back, and found herself against the wall. Undeterred, he came closer. She stiffened as his hand reached out to cup her throat. His fingers played on it a moment, then moved up past her face to bury themselves in her hair.

'Why not tonight?' he wanted to know.

It was hard to speak resolutely when the mere

act of breathing was a feat. 'You were very rude this morning.'

He laughed softly. 'I'll make you forget my rudeness.' He was so close to her now that she could feel his sweater against her cheek, and the tautness of his legs communicated itself to hers. She was glad of the wall at her back.

'Blye. . . .' she began.

'Time to talk later.'

He drew her to him, not seeming to notice that she tried to resist. The hand holding her head tilted it backward, supporting her neck at the same time. And then his mouth was descending to hers. She twisted away, and Blye found her throat instead. Sensuously he brushed his lips along the sensitive skin, trailing a path that set fire to her bloodstream. He found the hollow at the base of her throat, and let his tongue linger for a moment on the madly-beating pulse.

And then his lips were moving again, upwards, dancing kisses on her throat as he made for her mouth. He met with no resistance this time. Nicola was unable to suppress her trembling as his lips closed on hers. She was no longer thinking as she responded, willingly, with an ardour she had not known she possessed.

It was his turn to stiffen, as if the extent of her passion took him by surprise. Then the embrace tightened. His hands began to move over her, drawing her ever closer to him, moulding the small soft form to his own hard one. Nicola felt his hands shape themselves on her hips, then to her waist, then they were moving upwards to slide beneath her sweater. As a hand cupped a breast, she gave a small shudder of shock—shock that changed to helpless delight as Blye began an erotic stroking. Of her own accord she arched towards him.

Longing was a hard knot inside her, so that when he drew the sweater over her head she did nothing to stop him. Nor did she resist when he undid the clasp of her bra.

He stood a little away from her, looking down at her, and she saw the worship in his eyes. 'My darling, Nicola, you're lovely,' he groaned.

You're lovely too. Lovely in a way I never imagined. And I love you.

Love! She stared at him in fresh shock. She could not love him. She had decided not to love him.

But she did.

He did not seem to notice her shock. Almost reverently he touched her breasts once more, and as the nipples swelled and hardened into his fingers she heard his breathing quicken.

Without a word he undid the zip of her jeans. She stepped out of them. Then he lifted her in his arms. She could feel the beating of his heart against her cheek, hard, quick, and she knew that he wanted her as much as she wanted him. The knowledge gave a heady sensation all its own.

Gently he put her down on the bed and knelt down beside her, his eyes never leaving her. They lingered on a narrow waist and flat stomach, on legs that were shapely and smooth, on hips that curved with unconscious provocation, on firm breasts with nipples that said more than words could say. And then his eyes went to her face, and she saw in them an expression that was her undoing.

'Blye. . . .' There was no inhibition in her as she put her arms out to him.

His sweater came off, and then he was bending to her. His chest was rough and muscled on hers, and her hands slid over his back, learning the shape of the hard lines and angles, glorying in them.

Now when he kissed her there was no reserve. There was just a wonderful meeting of lips and arms, and they explored each other as if they could never get enough.

When Blye sat up Nicola stared at him dazed. 'You're beautiful,' he said.

Happiness was a tangible thing inside her. She could only look back at him.

'I want you, Nicola.'

'You have me,' she whispered.

There was a new expression on his face as he said, 'Not like this.'

'Blye. . . .'

'Nicola, we're both adults. And I want you.'

The moment of truth—and she did not know how to deal with it.

'You want me too, Nicola.'

Yes. Oh yes, yes! So badly. Because I love you. But you don't feel a thing for me, and I'm confused.

'Blye, perhaps. . . .' She stopped. Perhaps what? She did not know herself.

In a daze she watched as he began to unbuckle the belt of his trousers. On the periphery of her mind there was a knocking sound that had been going on a few moments.

'You do want me,' he insisted.

Yes, said her body, no, said her mind. There was also the knowledge that if she withdrew from Blye now she would make herself very foolish in his eyes. Eyes wide and troubled, she looked at him.

The knocking sounded again, and for the first time Nicola understood what it was—someone was knocking at her door. Blye's hands stopped on his belt. He looked towards the door, his eyes narrowed. 'It's very late.'

'I know. . . .'

The knocking sounded again.

'Ignore it,' Blye whispered.

'I can't.' Lifting herself on one elbow, Nicola called, 'Who is it?'

'Ella Barnes.' The voice came disconnectedly through the door.

Nicola looked around her and saw nothing within reach that she could put on. Cheeks burning—stupid that, for until this moment it had not bothered her that she was naked—she got off the bed, snatched a nightie from a drawer, then went to the door. Shielding the opening so that the woman could not see inside, she said, 'Mrs Barnes, what is it?'

'I don't feel well. I'm sorry to wake you so late, Nicola, but I'm not well.'

'Go back to your room, I'll be with you in a moment.'

Nicola closed the door and turned. Blye was no longer on the bed. He was standing. He had fastened his belt, but his chest was still bare, and the dim light caught it, highlighting its strong lines.

A low roar sounded through the night. A lion. Calling to its mate? Nicola shivered. Blye was a little like the lion, the jungle king, venerated and respected by all who came in contact with him. He had the same aura of power, of sheer maleness. In the daylight, when his eyes were blue and alert, he radiated intelligence and

authority. At this moment he was purely
physical. His sexuality seemed to reach to the
depths of her being even when there was no
actual contact between them.

'Mrs Barnes—she's not well.'

'I heard.'

Nicola made a little gesture of helplessness.
'I'm sorry.'

'Go to her, Nicola.'

She looked at him, caught by something in his
tone which she did not understand. 'I didn't plan
this.'

'Of course not.'

'Then why do you sound so mocking? As if . . .
as if I'd arranged for her to come just then. . . .'

'Because you might as well have done.'

Very deliberately, Nicola began to put on her
clothes. Without looking at Blye, she said, 'I
don't understand.'

'Mrs Barnes is as good an excuse as any other.'

'An excuse?' she repeated unsteadily.

'You needed one, didn't you?' No mistaking
the mockery now. 'If Mrs Barnes hadn't come
along you would have had to come up with
something else.'

Was it possible to love a man and to hate him
at the same time? Till today Nicola would have
said the answer was no. Now she was no longer
sure. It was not the only certainty which had
unexpectedly crumbled.

'You *are* arrogant,' she said in a low voice.

'And you, little Nicola, are a virgin.'

A statement, without expression or emphasis.
Nicola's bra and sweater were back on, she was
buttoning her jeans. At Blye's words her hands
froze.

She swung round. 'How do you know?'

'I know.'

Bravely she met his gaze. 'I told you I was experienced.'

'There are some things a man can sense.'

How? How, Blye, how? I didn't refuse you. I meant to refuse, though heaven only knows if I'd have had the strength to do so in the end. Was I so inadequate?

Nicola's cheeks burned. It should not matter that Blye had been disappointed in her, but it did.

'Will you be here when I get back?' she asked.

'No.'

'Oh. . . .'

'You have your reprieve.'

He didn't sound too sad as he said it. Nicola's head jerked up. 'You'll be going to Gloria instead, I suppose?'

Blye gave a short laugh. 'Some questions are better left unasked.'

Maybe so. Yet somehow the words emerged, almost of themselves. 'Are you, Blye?'

He picked up his sweater, and she watched as he pulled it over his head, down over his chest. Just a few minutes ago she had been against his chest, getting to know the feel of it.

'Did you think my attentions were exclusive?'

So he was going to Gloria. Trying to push away the sudden and quite appalling feeling of jealousy, Nicola shifted her gaze. It would never do for Blye to see her eyes, even in this light he would know how much he had hurt her.

She managed a shrug. 'Actually I didn't give them any thought.' She was astonished that the lie came out so coolly. 'And I don't care one way or the other.'

She was unprepared for the fingers that went to her cheek, pushing a strand of hair backwards over her ear. Her breath lurched in her lungs.

'You don't?' Blye asked.

'Well, of course not.' She pulled away from him. 'What did *you* think?'

Leave him now, while I have the last word. And wish the last word didn't sound quite so hollow in my own ears.

'I'll be off,' she said coolly, giving no pause for his answer. 'See yourself out, Mrs Barnes must be waiting.'

'I'm sure she is,' Blye responded politely. 'Sleep well, Nicola.'

Nicola did not respond as she walked through the door and pulled it closed with a bang. As she walked through the sweet-smelling darkness towards Mrs Barnes's bungalow she knew that if what had happened tonight would rob her of her sleep, it would not affect Blye's in the least.

The lion roared again. It was a spine-tingling sound, but Nicola was not frightened. The lion was out there in the dark, hunting perhaps, but she was in no danger from it. Her danger lay elsewhere. In a man with a ruggedly attractive face and a long hard body. A man with an appeal that was so devastating that he had become the centre of her mind.

As recently as this morning she had thought the appeal was purely physical, that what she felt for Blye was a chemical attraction that would vanish with the end of the tour and the parting of ways. Now she knew otherwise. She had fallen in love with Blye Peterson, and though he was arrogant and domineering and totally unworthy of her love she knew it would be very hard to forget him. Hard? Probably impossible.

CHAPTER SIX

NICOLA slept that night, but not well. When she awoke she remembered her dreams. 'Idiot,' she said fiercely to her reflection in the mirror. 'How can you be so foolish!'

When they met outside the bus one glance at Blye revealed that his own sleep had been undisturbed. He looked as alert and attractive as ever, his eyes sparkled when he looked at her and his skin had a glow, as if he'd risen early and spent some time out of doors. A little sourly Nicola wondered if he'd enjoyed himself with Gloria last night—and was sorry moments later that she had allowed the thought to enter her mind, for the vision that accompanied it brought a knifing pain. Swiftly she turned away from Blye and began an animated conversation with the Slades, who had just boarded.

Minutes later Mrs Barnes made her appearance, and now Nicola's talk was not forced at all. She was genuinely concerned about the elderly woman, and glad that she had been able to help her the night before.

She was moving among the passengers when Derek caught her hand. 'The Slades and possibly some of the others are coming to my room for drinks tonight. Join us.'

She shook her head. 'I can't.'

'After the braai. Please come, Nicola!'

'I'm sorry, Derek, I can't.'

'The tyrant been after you again?'

Involuntarily she glanced at Blye, and saw that he was watching her. It was impossible that he could have heard what was being said, nevertheless Nicola had the distinct impression that he'd caught the gist of it. Judging by the flint in his eyes, he disapproved.

Lifting her chin, she smiled at Derek, and wondered if Blye understood that the little gesture of defiance was directed purely at himself. 'My own decision, Derek. I'm sorry.'

It was a pleasant morning, with many animals, perfect opportunities for camera shots. It was a contented group of people who made their way back to camp.

In the time before lunch they relaxed on the lawns of the camp-grounds. Some stood at the fence, looking towards the river in search of game, others took photos.

Nicola noticed the honeymooners not far away. Maria, the young wife, stood by a frangipani, her expression poised and expectant as her husband focused his camera. When he had taken the photo they changed places, and she took one of him. They were about to walk away when Nicola went to them. Gesturing—for she was unable to converse with them—she indicated that she would like to take a photo of both of them together. 'Ah!' They were happy. Nicola quickly clicked three photos of the smiling and very-much-in-love pair.

'Nicola!' A call from Jim Slade as she was walking away from the Mavronis. 'You're a great little photographer. How about one of May and myself?'

'With pleasure,' Nicola assented, and when she'd complied, she said to Mrs Barnes, who was

Say Hello to Yesterday
Holly Weston had done it all alone.

She had raised her small son and worked her way up to features writer for a major newspaper. Still the bitterness of the the past seven years lingered.

She had been very young when she married Nick Falconer—but old enough to lose her heart completely when he left. Despite her success in her new life, her old one haunted her.

But it was over and done with—until an assignment in Greece brought her face to face with Nick, and all she was trying to forget. . . .

Time of the Temptress
The game must be played his way!

Rebellion against a cushioned, controlled life had landed Eve Tarrant in Africa. Now only the tough mercenary Wade O'Mara stood between her and possible death in the wild, revolution-torn jungle.

But the real danger was Wade himself—he had made Eve aware of herself as a woman.

"I saved your neck, so you feel you owe me something," Wade said. "But you don't owe me a thing, Eve. Get away from me." She knew she could make him lose his head if she tried. But that wouldn't solve anything. . . .

Your Romantic Adventure Starts Here.

Born Out of Love
It had to be coincidence!

Charlotte stared at the man through a mist of confusion. It was Logan. An older Logan, of course, but unmistakably the man who had ravaged her emotions and then abandoned her all those years ago.

She ought to feel angry. She ought to feel resentful and cheated. Instead, she was apprehensive—terrified at the complications he could create.

"We are not through, Charlotte," he told her flatly. "I sometimes think we haven't even begun."

Man's World
Kate was finished with love for good.

Kate's new boss, features editor Eliot Holman, might have devastating charms—but Kate couldn't care less, even if it was obvious that he was interested in her.

Everyone, including Eliot, thought Kate was grieving over the loss of her husband, Toby. She kept it a carefully guarded secret just how cruelly Toby had treated her and how terrified she was of trusting men again.

But Eliot refused to leave her alone, which only served to infuriate her. He was no different from any other man. . . or was he?

These FOUR free Harlequin Presents novels allow you to enter the world of romance, love and desire. As a member of the Harlequin Home Subscription Plan, you can continue to experience all the moods of love. You'll be inspired by moments so real...so moving...you won't want them to end. So start your own Harlequin Presents adventure by returning the reply card below. <u>DO IT TODAY!</u>

EXTRA BONUS
MAIL YOUR ORDER
TODAY AND GET A
FREE TOTE BAG
FROM HARLEQUIN.

also holding a camera, 'Let me take one of you. You'd look lovely beneath that flame-tree.'

She had just clicked when someone remarked, 'My goodness, is there no limit to your talents?' A sneering voice, unmistakable.

Very slowly Nicola put the camera back in the case. Only when she had her face under control did she lift her eyes to Gloria. 'No great talent needed to take photos,' she said smoothly.

'Ah, but such amiability. Cheerful service on and off duty. What a gem Delayney Tours have in you!'

'Thank you.' Nicola refused to rise to the bait. 'Perhaps you'd like a photo too.'

'No, thanks.' Perfect teeth gleamed in a rare smile. 'Blye will take it if I want one.' The smile widened. 'He sees to all my needs.'

Bitch! Silently Nicola sent the word across the air-waves to Gloria. Had they met in different circumstances there were things she would have said aloud to this impossible woman. As it was, all she could do was retain her dignity and be glad that when the tour ended she would not have to see Gloria again.

'Don't let her upset you,' Mrs Barnes said, when Gloria had walked away.

Several people seemed to have said that to her lately. Nicola shrugged. 'I'm not upset.'

'Horrid woman! And not as beautiful as her pictures.'

Nicola stared. 'I don't understand.'

'You don't know who she is?'

'Should I?'

Mrs Barnes gave a slightly shamefaced smile. 'It's obvious you don't read the gossip pages. Quite an unpleasant divorce she's been through. Dirty.'

'I didn't know. I'm surprised,' Nicola mused, 'that you recognised her.'

'Well, maybe I wouldn't have, but there was all the talk about Beldon Delayney being mixed up with her.'

'Beldon Delayney? Of Delayney Tours?'

'I should think so. It was the name that made me take notice of the case. I'd already booked the tour. What's he like, Nicola?'

'I've never met him.'

But she had been in his office. Vividly she remembered the occasion. Blye had seemed so confident as he'd written out the cheque at that elegant desk. She'd wondered then where he'd got the nerve to do it. Now she thought that perhaps he had known Mr Delayney was away and occupied with matters that had nothing to do with the affairs of the company.

Leaving Mrs Barnes, Nicola decided to go for a walk on her own. She was growing to love the camp-grounds. They were so colourful, the scarlet flame-trees contrasting joyously with fire-red hibiscus and bougainvillaea that ranged from purple to orange. Birds were everywhere. Nicola enjoyed the jays most; they squabbled on the ground, vivid blue and jewel-like, alert for every crumb they could find.

For once Nicola's attention was not on her immediate surroundings. She was reflecting on the facts Mrs Barnes had let slip. That Gloria was a society beauty who had been involved in a divorce that had made the newspapers was not altogether surprising. Gloria's combination of brittle good looks, superb figure and lovely clothes would make her an obvious target for the gossip columns of the press.

But what was the woman's interest in Blye? Did she see in him a link with Mr Delayney? Or had her interest in that gentleman waned once she had met the person who worked for him? The Delayney fortune would be a powerful lure to a woman like Gloria, yet perhaps Blye's undoubted sex appeal was more tempting still.

Unhappily Nicola had to admit to herself that Blye's physical appeal was a daunting force indeed.

At one end of the grounds was a clump of maroela trees, and drawn by the shade they offered Nicola decided to walk that way. She was in the trees when she saw she was not alone. Hidden till now by the trunk of a maroela was a figure she recognised. Happily Nicola moved forward. Silly not to talk to Blye, they might as well put an end to the tension that had existed between them all day.

He had his back to her, and did not seem to hear her approach. For once she was the silent one Nicola thought, and grinned. She came to a sudden halt. Two arms had wound themselves around Blye's neck, and then a golden-haired head was visible by his shoulder. Gloria! It could be nobody else.

Nicola's heart gave a painful jerk, and the blood left her checks as she put a hand out to a tree for support. Within moments she had recovered her composure. Leave the scene. Leave it quickly, before the two lovers became aware of her prescnce.

In her haste her foot struck a stone. It skittered into a rock, and the noise it made was very loud in the quietness of the trees.

Blye spun round, Gloria beside him. Nicola

stood quite still, her heart beating painfully fast. For a long moment her gaze and Blye's met and held.

Then Gloria drawled, 'Why, if it isn't the little tour-guide spying on us!' There was a look of triumph on her face—a most peculiar look. Nicola was too distraught to wonder at its cause.

'I wasn't spying!' she retorted.

'It certainly looks like it.'

'I'd gone for a walk. I didn't know. . . .'

She broke off. Blye was still watching her, his eyes narrowed. Gloria merely looked malicious. Suddenly Nicola was angry. Why, these two were making her feel guilty when she had done nothing wrong! Anger brought her strength, and her cheeks felt warm as the blood came surging back into them. Dropping her hand from the tree—she no longer needed the crutch—she took a step towards them.

'I didn't know I'd find you here,' she said steadily. 'And I'll leave you to your fun. But not before I tell you how disgusted I am.'

'Disgusted?' Blye's voice was odd.

'Right. Just yesterday you preached company policy to me. No fraternisation between tour guests and staff. Funny the rules don't apply to you, Blye Peterson!'

Blye opened his mouth to speak, but Gloria cut in before he could get the words out. 'Even you must know, Miss Goody Two-Shoes, that what applies to the staff doesn't hold good for the boss.'

'The boss?'

Nicola turned to Blye. The skin on his cheeks had tightened so that he looked more gaunt than usual, infinitely more stern. He put a hand on his companion's arm and said, 'Gloria, please!' but she ignored him, and repeated, maliciously, 'The boss.' She paused the merest fraction of a moment before continuing. 'Your boss, Nicola dear. Beldon Delayney.'

'That's impossible!' Nicola burst out shocked. 'It's not true!'

But perhaps it *is* true. Look at Blye's face. Grim, and pale despite his tan. He didn't want me to know, he alone knows why. And now Gloria's let it out. He lied to me. And I feel ill— even more ill than when I found out about Jonathan's perfidy.

'It's true,' Blye said steadily. 'I'm sorry, Nicola.'

'Why should you be sorry, Blye darling?' This from Gloria. 'You had your reasons. As for you, Nicola, I suppose what you've learned will affect your attitude.'

'It certainly will!'

'I thought so.' Honeyed tones. 'Most women are quite overawed by Beldon Delayney's position and money. Aren't they, darling? You'll have to watch yourself with little Nicola. She may just begin to think about you in a new way.'

'Darn right I will!' Shock and disillusionment had brought Nicola closer to tears than she wanted the pair to know. 'I do already. As far as I'm concerned I'm even more disgusted than I was a few minutes ago.'

What would they say to her now? Gloria with her triumphant expression; Blye Peterson— correction, Beldon Delayney—with a face that was a bleak mask. Would they castigate the novice tour-guide who had forgotten herself so far as to be rude to the big boss and his lady-friend? Nicola did not care what they said, what they thought. Without looking at either of them she turned on her heel and fled.

'Nicola!' Blye caught up with her as she was running to her bungalow.

'Leave me alone!'

'You're very shocked, and I'm sorry.'

Eyes blazing, she turned on him. 'You've got to be kidding! You've never been sorry for a thing in your entire life!'

The line of his jaw was inflexible. He had the look of a man who was making a great effort to control himself. 'We have to talk.'

'We've nothing to talk about!'

She heard him draw in his breath as he stepped forward and seized one of her wrists. Despite her fury her pulses began a sudden racing, and that fact made her even angrier.

'I left Gloria standing,' he said.

'Poor Gloria!'

'We do have to talk, Nicola.'

'Get your hands off me!' she threw the words at him. 'I can't stand you to touch me!'

A muscle moved in his throat, and something flickered briefly in the blue eyes. Then, unexpectedly, he seemed to relax. The corners of his lips lifted and into his face came an expression that was lazily outrageous. 'That wasn't my impression last night.'

He did not release her wrist, but his thumb began a slow stroking up and down the sensitive skin along the inside of her arm. Nicola had not thought her pulses could beat any faster, but they did. 'Last night was different,' she managed.

'Because my name was different?'

Don't you know that I don't care about your

name? Blye Peterson, Beldon Delayney, Tom Smith, I'd love you no matter what your name is.

What *does* matter is that you are rich and powerful. That you think of me only as a diversion. I must have been utterly crazy to let myself believe, even for a moment, that you thought otherwise. And what matters is Gloria. I knew she was after you, but I didn't know that she was your mistress, that you were involved in her divorce.

'Well, Nicola?'

'Not only your name.'

The movement of his thumb was tantalising. It was enough to break the strongest resolve. Impossible to control a shudder.

'You're responding again,' he said softly.

'With revulsion.' She was proud that she was able to say it with spirit. 'You felt me tremble, I know. But if you think it was with passion you're flattering youself. Get your hands off me, Beldon Delayney!'

'Blye. And we do have to talk.' He cast a look in the direction of the maroelas. 'Gloria will be wondering. . . . Later, Nicola.'

'Forget it.' She pulled her wrist away from him and wished it didn't feel suddenly quite so bare. 'Get back to your lady-friend. We've nothing to say to each other!'

She refused to watch him as he walked away. She also decided against going to her room. That would be hiding. She would not hide—not from anybody.

Derek was standing at another part of the fence, binoculars to his eyes as he scanned the bush for game. 'Nicola!' he looked around pleased at her approach.

'Spot anything?'

'Yeah—a dozen lions.'

'Fantastic.' She gave a little laugh at the joke and hoped that he did not hear its unsteadiness. 'Invitation still open for tonight?'

'The party? You bet!'

'Thanks. I've changed my mind about it. I'd like to come.'

'I'm glad.' Exuberantly he hugged her to him. Through the thin fabric of her safari-style shirt she could feel his fingers flat against her waist.

I feel nothing, Nicola thought. Absolutely nothing. Will it always be like this with any man other than Blye?

'Great wine,' Nicola giggled. 'More, please, Derek.'

'Sure, honey, sure.'

She giggled again as she watched the amber liquid pour into the glass. Was this the nectar that the gods had drunk? Once she got used to the dry taste it was delicious. She sloshed the glass around, watching the wine bubble, then drank it, quickly, in one long sip.

'More,' she said to Derek.

'Sure,' he agreed, but May Slade put a hand on his arm. 'No, Derek—she's tipsy. Don't give her any more.'

Undeterred, Derek poured another glass and handed it to Nicola. 'Enjoy yourself, honey.'

Enjoy myself? asked a small voice deep inside her. I don't think I'll enjoy myself ever again. But you don't know that. Nobody does.

'I'm enjoying myself.' She leaned back, her head against his shoulder. His arm tightened around her, and she snuggled closer. Derek was nice, and he liked her—more than could be said for some she could think of.

'What would Blye Peterson say?' May worried.

'The ogre?' This from Derek. 'Why bother about him?'

'What Blye Peterson?' Nicola's words were slurred.

'Our driver.' May peered into her face. 'Blye Peterson. Oh dear, Nicola, you can't be that far gone!'

'No Blye Peterson.' Nicola snuggled even closer to Derek. 'Imaginary person.'

Derek gave a shout of delight. 'You're a great girl—fun. Wish you'd always be so relaxed.'

Playfully she tweaked his ear. 'Maybe I will be from now on.'

'Certainly a new slant on you, Nicola,' Jim remarked.

'I don't like it,' May fretted.

'Aw, come on,' Derek protested. 'Imaginary being or not, I wish Blye could see you now.'

Do you? Nicola wondered. He'd be furious. I may be drunk, but I'm not so drunk I don't know that.

'Stuffy fellow. Should have heard him go on about company regulations!'

'What company regulations?' Nicola murmured. She giggled again. 'No company regulations. Not any more.'

'That's my girl!'

'All imaginary. Like Blye.'

Jim began to sing.

> *'It's a long way to Tipperary,*
> *It's a long way to go.'*

The others joined in.

> *'It's a long way to Tipperary,*
> *To the sweetest girl I know.'*

Nicola's head was throbbing, and she felt a little ill, but she sang, waving her glass, her head still against Derek's shoulder.

> *'Goodbye, Piccadilly, Farewell Leicester*
> *Square. . . .'*

The door flung open and the song stopped abruptly. Blye strode into the room. 'What's going on here?' he demanded.

'A party,' said Derek.

'And you weren't invited.' Nicola's giggle was more high-pitched than before.

'Come along.' Blye addressed himself solely to Nicola, who was still huddled against Derek.

'Oh dear, I knew there'd be trouble,' groaned May. 'Blye, go easy.'

'Not Blye,' Nicola interrupted. 'A ghost. I can see right through him. Go 'way ghost.'

Face tight and cold, Blye turned on Derek. 'You made her drunk!'

'Get out of here, Peterson.'

'Get your hands off her. Now!'

'I want more wine,' said Nicola. 'Derek please.'

'Sure, honey.' He poured it, was handing it to her when Blye took it from his hand and put it firmly down on the table. Nicola was not so far gone that she did not see the controlled passion in the long fingers. He wants to strike out at something, she thought.

'Hey now, listen,' Derek protested. 'Aren't you forgetting your position here? You're only the driver here.'

'I'm forgetting nothing.' Blye's tone was taut. 'If you weren't a paid guest on this tour I'd have thrown this glass through the door and you'd have gone head-first behind it. Come along, Nicola.'

'She's enjoying herself.' Derek's hand tightened on her shoulders. 'Get the hell out of here, Peterson!'

'With Nicola.'

Without warning Blye reached for Nicola's hand and pulled her easily away from Derek. He did not release her as he made for the door.

Perhaps Derek was stunned, or perhaps he was intimidated by a strength that was obviously greater than his own. Either way, he made no move to stop Blye. In the moment before the door closed behind them she heard May wail yet again, 'Oh, I knew there'd be trouble!'

It had been warm in Derek's bungalow. The cold night air was a shock. Nicola felt suddenly very weak, her legs so watery that she could not take another step. She stopped.

'Get moving,' Blye ordered.

'I can't.'

'You can.'

'Don't bully me, Blye . . . I mean Beldon.'

'Blye. And I'll bully you all I please. Come along, Nicola.'

'I can't,' she whispered. 'Oh, Blye, I feel awful!'

Without warning her legs buckled and she sank on to the ground. Above her Blye towered, powerful and savage in the moonlight. For a long moment he looked down at her, his face set and unfeeling. Then he bent and scooped her into his arms as easily as if she was a rag doll.

'Put me down,' she demanded unsteadily.

'In your room.'

'Here. I don't want to be in your arms.'

I'm lying. I do want it. Even now, knowing what I know. Am I crazy? Is this what love does to one? If it is, I'm sorry I ever set eyes on you.

'And I don't want our guests to see their drunken tour-guide in a stupor on the grass.' There was no sympathy in his tone. No hint of affection or understanding. Beldon Delayney's sole concern was for the reputation of his company. His help meant no more than that.

Yet even that knowledge did not stop the feeling of pleasure that being in his arms gave her. She was confused and angry, and the unaccustomed wine had made her feel ill, but she could still enjoy the hardness of his chest against her cheek, the roughness of his sweater, the steely tightness of his arms.

This was not how she had wanted things to be between them. She wanted more, so very much more than Blye would ever know, more than it was in him to give—at least to Nicola Sloane, who was just an underling in a very large company. And yet she wished that the walk to her bungalow was further, that she remain longer in his arms.

I wouldn't have stood this from Jonathan, she thought. Why do I take it from Blye? Have I really sunk so low? And oh, I don't feel well. I don't feel well at all.

'I don't feel well,' she told him as they came to her bungalow.

'Serves you right.' He pushed open the door and carried her inside.

Like a bride—the thought flashed through her mind. A radiant bride being carried over the threshold by her doting husband. Her lips twisted painfully.

A second later she was dumped none too gently on her bed by a man who was not doting at all.

'So you feel awful.'

'Yes.'

'I'd like to give Derek a hiding! He had no right to make you drunk.'

'Don't blame Derek,' she protested. She looked up at Blye, then flinched as she wished she hadn't. He was extraordinarily handsome tonight; his sweater matched his eyes and his anger made the rugged face more vital than ever.

'Light hurting you?' he asked.

'Yes,' she lied, then said again, 'Don't blame Derek. I invited myself to the party. I wanted the wine.'

'He saw what it did to you. He knew very well you were getting drunk.'

'Not drunk—tipsy. May Slade said I was tipsy.'

'Drunk,' Blye repeated flatly. 'Wine, Nicola? That's all you had?'

'Yes. People don't get drunk on wine.'

'When they're not used to it they do.' His laughter rang out suddenly, deep and amused.

'What's so funny?' she asked crossly.

'You, my love. You're just a baby, aren't you? And you try so hard to prove that you're not.'

'I don't know what you're talking about,' she said stiffly.

'An innocent virgin who pretends to be sophisticated in the ways of men. And an innocent young woman for whom social drinking is too much. Why did you do it, Nicola?'

'I wanted to. Don't tower like that, it makes me feel giddy, Blye. . . .' She stopped. 'But you're not Blye. I'll have to remember to call you Beldon.'

'Blye.' He was impatient. 'I've told you that before. I've always been called Blye.'

'And I suppose your surname was always Peterson.'

'No. Delayney is my real name.'

'Strange,' she said reflectively, 'you don't even look ashamed.'

'I'm not. Though I am sorry.'

Sorry? He looked like some ancient pagan god, rugged and virile, dwarfing the room with the sheer power of his personality. Nicola did not believe Blye—Peterson or Delayney—had ever been sorry, truly sorry, in his life.

'I don't believe you.' She hunched herself up in the bed, the better to demonstrate her defiance. Unprepared for the dizziness that assailed her she put a hand to her eys. 'I feel ill.'

'Sure you do.' His voice was more gentle than it had been. 'We'll talk about my name and all that goes with it tomorrow.'

'I'm not interested. . . .'

'You'll hear it anyway. Now let's get you to bed.'

She looked at him in alarm. 'I can manage on my own, thank you. Goodnight, Blye.'

'I'll go when you're in bed.'

She firmed her tone to say, 'This is ridiculous,' and was immediately sorry as her voice echoed in her head. 'You can leave now,' she said more quietly.

'When you're in bed.' His manner brooked no argument. 'You're in no state to manage on your own.'

He was absolutely right. Getting out of her clothes, brushing her teeth, the simple functions of getting to bed, were feats that seemed too enormous even to contemplate. She would stay as she was, she would sleep in her clothes.

'For heaven's sake!' Helplessness made her angry.

'You're not going to sleep in your uniform.'

How did he know that had been her intention? But Blye had always known everything, right from the start.

'The precious Delayney uniform,' she sneered. 'It wouldn't do to get it crumpled.'

'It wouldn't do for you to lie all night on top of your bed,' he said evenly. 'It gets very cold, you know that. You'd be sick by tomorrow.'

'As if you'd care!'

He grinned mockingly. 'Don't you know the tour needs its guide?'

Oh, he was horrible! Nicola raised herself once more, the better to tell him what she thought of him, and fell back.

He laughed softly. 'You can say it all tomorrow. Besides, I do care. Don't you know that, Nicola?'

It made no sense that her heart quickened. So he cared. What of it? Anyone who was not quite inhuman would care about a fellow being who was ill. That did not make the caring a special thing. Besides, there was Gloria. . . .

'I don't know,' she murmured.

'All the more reason for me to wait while you get into bed.'

The heartbeat increased. 'Why did you lie to me, Blye?'

Was it her imagination, or did his jaw tighten? But his tone unchanged. 'We'll talk tomorrow. Get out of your clothes, Nicola.'

'When you've gone.'

'Now!' The word had the sound of unyielding authority.

'Turn your back, then,' she commanded weakly.

He laughed again, and the sound was so seductive that her raw nerves seemed on fire. 'I like the view.'

'Blye!'

'The innocent virgin again. All right then, Nicola, let me see you get up and make a start. After that I'll direct my eyes to the wall.'

Nicola took one breath, then another. She wished her head was just a little clearer, that her limbs felt a part of her body. Discipline, she told herself, that's all I need.

Keeping her eyes firmly away from Blye, she pulled herself to a sitting position. As the dizziness came over her once more she nearly swayed; only her resolve kept her vertical.

Involuntarily she looked across at Blye. He was standing by the wall, one long leg leaning nonchalantly across the other. Very politely he met her gaze. He showed no sign of turning.

He'd meant what he'd said. He wanted proof that she could cope on her own, and no argument would deflect him. Could anything deflect him from his purpose ever? Besides, she was in no state to argue.

Concentrating hard, she lifted her right hand in the direction of the top button of her sweater. The hand wavered, rose slightly, fell. Strange that it could not make contact, she had never had similar trouble before.

Dazed, she shook a head that seemed filled with cotton candy. Helplessly she looked at Blye, and felt herself falling.

He caught her. One arm supported her back,

the other was holding her against him, and she felt the rough sweater again.

'How many glasses of wine did you have?' she heard him ask against her hair.

'Three, maybe four.'

'My innocent girl!' He was laughing, his breath warming her cheek, his chest shaking against her. 'Oh, Nicola, what am I going to do with you?'

'Why don't you just let me die?'

A new gust of laughter bubbled in his throat. 'It might be easier to put you to bed.'.

Was that so funny? Perhaps in the morning, when she felt better—would she ever feel better?—she might understand the joke. Right now there was just the appalling knowledge that Blye really meant what he said. Worse still, there was very little she could do to stop him.

CHAPTER SEVEN

NICOLA was quite still as Blye began to remove
her clothes. She lay with her eyes averted.
Everything had gone wrong. She loved him and
he did not love her. After tonight she would no
longer even have his affection and respect. He
would leave her, and he would go to Gloria, and
before they made love he would tell the vicious
blonde woman what had happened and they
would laugh together. Nicola would be an object
of ridicule in their eyes after that. It was not to be
borne.

And there was nothing she could do about it. If
only she had not been so foolish as to drink the
wine! May Slade had said it would lead to
trouble, and so it had.

Derek was not to blame. Nicola had invited
herself to the party and asked for the wine. If she
was old enough to be a tour-guide she was old
enough to take care of herself. It was unforgivable
that she had allowed anger and jealousy to make
her ill.

The jacket was off, the slacks too, and Blye was
sliding a hand beneath her back to unfasten her
bra. Nicola made a move to stop him, but he
brushed her away.

And then he was standing by the bed, looking
down at her. The laughter that had been in his
eyes was now gone.

'My darling, Nicola, you're beautiful.' The words
emerged on a groan.

'Blye,' she whispered.

A hand reached out and touched her throat, lingered briefly on the hollow at its base, then trailed gently down. It touched one breast, traced a path around it, then moved to the other. And all the while Nicola could not move her eyes from his, and it was hard to breathe.

'Why do you have to be so beautiful?' He bent down suddenly, and she felt his lips touch the spots where his fingers had been.

'You want to make love to me?' The words were out without thinking.

'Any man with red blood in his veins and eyes in his head would want to make love to you.'

I don't want any other man. I just want you. I love you, don't you know that?

'Do you want to?' she whispered.

'The teasing of the innocent.' His tone was so harsh that she winced. 'Don't step out of your league till you're ready to, Nicola. Leave that to the experts.'

Gloria. Gloria was the expert. What would he want with Nicola when he could have Gloria?

'It was just a question,' she muttered.

'All right then, I'll give you your answer. I do want to make love to you, but I won't. I don't make a practice of seducing young virgins, especially when they're too drunk to know what they're doing.'

'Gloria would know what she's doing.' Why did she have to torture herself? Just saying the words was painful, and yet some defiance seemed called for.

'Precisely.' The sensuous lips thinned. 'What do you sleep in, Nicola, or do you sleep in the nude?'

Her nightie was under her pillow. Blye pulled it over her head, his movements rougher than when he had undressed her. He was angry, and Nicola wished she knew why.

He covered her with the blanket, and looked down at her once more. There was no softness in his face now. 'Sleep it off,' he said without expression. 'I'll see you in the morning.'

Not even a goodnight. With a heavy heart she watched him walk out and close the door. Where was he going? To Gloria? Silly of her even to wonder, the answer was so obvious.

Painfully Nicola moved her aching head on the pillow, searching for a comfortable position. She would not sleep tonight, she knew that, and tomorrow she would feel even worse.

But she had underestimated the effects of four glasses of wine. When the door opened twenty minutes later she did not hear it.

Blye came to her bed. He stood beside it, looking down. On his face was a curious expression, a brooding tautness mixed with a kind of wonderment. It was an expression that Nicola would have been at a loss to explain had she seen it.

He put out his hand and smoothed a damp tendril of hair from her forehead. Then he bent. To kiss her? Had she been awake she could not have answered that question either, for he straightened abruptly without touching her. As he made for the door he said something under his breath.

It was the aroma of coffee that woke her. She lay savouring it for a moment, her eyes still closed. And then a thought came into her head, and her eyes fluttered quickly open. As she looked at the tall figure just a yard from her bed her cheeks grew hot.

'What are you doing here?'

'Good morning, Blye,' he mocked. 'It's so nice to see you, Blye. And oh, how very thoughtful of you to bring me such a nice hot cup of coffee!'

'What are you doing here?' she muttered.

'As you see—I brought you coffee.'

'You've never done that before,' she observed suspiciously, thinking at the same time how very handsome he looked. His hair was damp and glossy, as if he had very recently stepped from a shower, and the gaunt face had a freshness that made her want to reach out and caress it.

'I've never had a tour-guide with a hangover before.' His response was mild.

She gave voice to a niggling worry. 'Am I still a tour-guide?'

'Why do you ask?'

'I thought perhaps . . . after last night. . . .'

'You deserve a good spanking, and if you don't take the coffee I might just haul you out of bed and administer a few strokes.' His eyes gleamed.

'You wouldn't dare!' she exclaimed.

'Wouldn't I?' he asked with such relish that she hastily took the cup he held out to her.

She took a sip; the coffee was good. Blye watched her in silence. It was only when she looked up that he said, 'To answer your question—of course you're still a tour-guide.'

'Oh!' She tried not to show her relief.

'I wouldn't like to lose you.'

You couldn't lose me if you tried. You've captured my heart and my mind, the parts of me that think and feel. I have an awful feeling that

you'll always have them, even when the tour has
ended and you have passed out of my life. I
wonder if there will be a time when you do not
occupy my thoughts during the day and my
dreams at night.

'You're good at your job,' he went on.

That's all I am to you—an employee who's
good at her job.

Her hand shook.

'You'll spill and get burned,' he observed. 'Sit
up, Nicola.'

She knew she had to sit, it was hard to drink
from an almost prone position. But it was no easy
matter to prop herself up when she was holding a
brimming cup in one hand while with the other
she tried to keep the blanket beneath her chin.

He gave a shout of laughter. 'You're unreal!'

'What have I done to amuse you now?' Nicola
asked stiffly, knowing exactly the cause of his
laughter.

'Any Victorian ancestors you might possess
would be proud of you. Do you think the animal
in me will emerge if I see a suggestion of throat
or even, heaven forbid, the swell of a pretty
breast? Nicola, my darling, I've seen you in less.'

Her heart thudded at the endearment. A quick
glance at his face showed its utter lack of
significance. Darling—it was the kind of word
people used casually, often in amusement. Gloria
at her most venomous might say, 'Nicola darling,
I don't know how Delayney Tours ever managed
without you.'

'Me and others,' she said, a little crossly.

'Jealous?' The word was a seductive drawl.

'Me? Good gracious, no, you really do like to
flatter yourself, Blye, I mean Beldon Delayney.'

'Blye,' he corrected her softly.

'Blye, then. I don't care how many women you've slept with. What concerns me is your behaviour.'

'Ah!'

'You lied to me.'

'I told you we'd discuss it this morning.'

'You've had plenty of time to think, up a fantastic excuse.'

She wanted so badly to be in his arms, to draw his head down on to her breast, that it was hard to be angry at him. She wondered what his excuse would be, hoped it would be one that was easy to forgive.

And that was ridiculous. She was letting the sensuousness of the moment overwhelm her. It would have been better by far to have this conversation in a sterile businesslike atmosphere. In the bus perhaps, facing each other across the cold leather seats. Instead, here she was in her flimsy nightie, lying in the bed where just hours ago she had been undressed by a man who was more attractive than any man should have the right to be.

'I've thought up nothing,' said Blye. 'I'll just tell you the truth.'

It was her turn to say 'Ah!'

'Nicola.' He took her hand.

There was a familiar tingling which she tried to ignore. She was a modern girl with heaps of self-respect and a mind of her own. Blye had behaved badly, and the fact that she loved him did not excuse him.

She pulled her hand away. 'That will get you nowhere,' she said coolly. 'You lied to me, Blye. After telling me that there were to be no more lies between us.'

'Right. . . .'

'My own lies—goodness, they weren't lies, they were tiny falsehoods—were nothing in comparison.'

'Are you going to let me talk?' He had the nerve to look unruffled.

'Yes, why don't you.' Even icier. 'And don't leave anything out.'

'You know most of it already. My name is Beldon Delayney and I own Delayney Tours.'

'Among other things.'

'Among other things,' he agreed pleasantly. 'And in a few minutes I shall want to know why that fact should make you quite so bitter. Right then, Nicola, why did I call myself Peterson? I'd have thought it was obvious—so that I can be incognito.'

'Is that necessary?'

'Sometimes. I like to move informally around the different concerns, see things from other perspectives. If I'm not known—and to many of my employees I'm only a name—it makes it easier.'

'Easier to spy on people!'

'I don't spy,' he countered impatiently. 'It's as I just said, I like to see things from another perspective. Not only from my vantage point as the president of Delayney Corporation.'

'From the employee's seat.'

'Right.'

'The king, moving around his kingdom, hobnobbing with the commoners. Returning to the palace when he tires of the drudgery.'

'Try to understand,' urged Blye. 'A long time ago, my father insisted that I work my way up from the bottom. That I knew each step of the ladder before I progressed to the next. It made sense then, it still does now.'

'You've finished your climb, Blye,' Nicola told him.

'The concept hasn't lost its meaning. It's a good captain, Nicola, who understands what his sailors do—really understands. So that he knows what his orders mean to them, what they can and cannot do. And it's only by working with them that he sees how matters can be changed and improved. This is one hell of a long speech, Nicola. You must be bored.'

'You have me drinking in every word.' She said it sarcastically, knowing that he would accept it as such. Yet really she was telling the truth. She loved to hear him talk, and she was infinitely impressed with his dedication and innovativeness.

'The day I came for the interview—you were doing a stint in Personnel?'

'Yes.'

'And when John was taken ill—you'd been waiting for a chance to drive a tour?'

He hesitated just a fraction of a moment, but when he spoke his tone was smooth. 'That's right.'

'What about the name? Did you blindfold yourself and wave a pencil over a page in the telephone directory?'

'I've always been called Blye—short for Beldon. Peterson was my mother's maiden name.'

It was all so simple. Too simple.

'Do you understand that my subterfuge wasn't directed at you personally?' he asked.

'I suppose so.'

'Then why the bitterness?'

What Nicola felt at this moment was anything but bitterness. Rather her emotions had to do with the part of her that was essentially female, a primeval response to an intoxicating maleness. The coffee was long finished, and still she sat propped against the pillow, for to crawl back beneath the blanket would be to invite Blye's attention and ridicule. He was such a presence in the small room—tall and broad and exuding a virile vitality that was uniquely his own. He made her feel smaller, a little vulnerable. He also filled her with a longing that made rational thought very hard.

And yet she *must* think rationally, must keep her wits about her, give him answers that made sense.

'Yesterday you implied that there was more to your bitterness than the name,' he prompted, seemingly unaware of the effect he was having on her.

'Your money.'

'My money!' He was astonished.

'You're so rich.'

'And that upsets you?' He was looking at her oddly. 'It seems to send most of the women I know into raptures.'

So that he did not know if he was liked for his money or for himself? And was Gloria one of those women? Surely Blye must know the extent of his sex-appeal, that he was far above and beyond most mortal men.

'I hate the place money has in a relationship.' Nicola bit her lip and looked away. She was letting his nearness get to her, so that she spoke without thinking. There was no relationship—at least not as far as Blye was concerned.

'Go on.'

A look at his face showed that he expected her to finish what she was saying. 'My engagement broke up because of money. I had none and Anthea had lots, and Jonathan found it was as easy to love a rich woman as a poor one.'

'We're not engaged, Nicola, and I'm not tempted by a rich woman.' The lazy drawl was insolent. 'Yet you presume to judge me by Jonathan.'

Her cheeks flamed. 'I was telling you why money upsets me.'

He was silent as he looked down at her. In the dim light of the bungalow she could not read his eyes, yet for some reason her heart began to beat even faster. Finding that she could not sustain his gaze, she shifted her eyes—and jerked as her chin was caught by his hand and her head was turned gently, yet firmly, on the pillow.

'An unfair comparison,' Blye said softly when he had forced her to look at him once more.

'I wasn't comparing.' Her pulsebeat was so rapid that she felt sure he must feel it where his fingers touched her throat.

'I wasn't comparing,' she said again, bumpily.

'Jonathan was looking for money,' he went on as if he had not heard the protest. 'I happen to have money, Nicola, I don't need a woman to give me more.'

'I know, I was just. . . .'

'What else upsets you about me?'

He was relentless. She should have known he would be a powerful adversary before she decided to take him on. 'Your status,' she said.

'I *am* flattered.' His tone was dry.

He was baiting her, damn him.

'You're a big name in the business world, a tycoon.'

'So?'

'And I. . . . I'm a tour-guide. A novice guide at that.

'I can't believe we're talking class system. That went out years ago.'

'Did it?' She threw the question at him. 'You belong in one world, Blye, you and Gloria. Champagne for breakfast and caviar for dinner. What do you know about people who eat hamburgers, who look for ways to stretch the last of their cash till the next pay-day comes along? Did you enjoy giving me the cheque? It was your money, wasn't it? But you pretended it came from Delayney Tours.'

'As it happened it did. And I know about people who eat hamburgers. What are you trying to say, Nicola?'

'You touch me. You kiss me and pretend to find me desirable. . . .'

'I do find you desirable.' He grinned as he bent towards her.

She felt the beginnings of a treacherous response, but she twisted away. 'Don't change the subject!'

'It's an extremely pleasant one.'

He found her desirable! The words thundered in her ears, in her heart.

Don't get carried away, for heaven's sake! Not now. Later, alone, I can remember the words and enjoy them. Cherish them, even.

'That's not the point,' she managed, shakily.

'Isn't it?' His eyes glinted wickedly. 'And you, my adorable Nicola, find me desirable too.'

'You're awfully conceited!' She couldn't help laughing.

'Awfully,' he agreed. 'You do, Nicola, don't you?'

'A little,' she conceded, knowing she could hardly do otherwise—her body had spoken for her too often. 'But it *isn't* the point, Blye, it really isn't.'

'What is, then?'

If only he would straighten, retreat some way. He was so close to her that she felt quite giddy.

'That you despise me,' she said in a low voice.

'Despise!' The word exloded through the room with its pointed thatched ceiling.

'I'm just one more of your employees. You enjoy playing with me, and at the same time you despise me.'

'How very illuminating!' His voice was as mocking as she'd heard it. 'I take it you really believe what you're saying.'

The expression on the rugged face was a taunt. Nicola quivered, but she held her ground. 'Yes, I do.'

'I'll have to show you just how much I despise you.'

This time when he swooped there was no escaping him. He had caught her in his arms before she could move. He kissed her with a tantalising lightness, then he lifted his head and looked down at her, it was hard to breathe as she looked back at him. His fingers reached for her face and began to trail a path around her lips, and then her eyes and around her temples. There was tenderness in the touch, and a sweetness that was more intoxicating than anything Nicola had ever known.

'This wasn't what I intended when I brought you the coffee,' he said softly.

Her breathing was shallow. 'Wasn't it?'

A hand slid beneath the neckline of her nightie and found first one breast, then the other. And still the movement was light, sensuously light.

'I just meant to wake you,' he whispered.

You have woken me, my darling Blye. You've woken a sleeping girl from her dreams and plunged her into the emotions and needs of womanhood, and I love you for it. But I despair even more, because I know it can't last—not with you—and I don't know if I'll ever be able to recapture anything even remotely like it with someone else.

'Liar,' she said shakily.

'How could you think I despise you?' She had never heard his voice so ragged. 'You're so lovely, Nicola, how could any man despise you?'

For answer she touched his hair, buried her fingers in it, let herself enjoy the thick smoothness.

'Do you know what you're doing to me?' he groaned.

Instinct, pure feminine instinct, drove her. 'What?'

'Witch—lovely, desirable little witch. I'll show you what you're doing, Nicola.'

He gathered her to him, closer this time, so that she could feel the thudding of a heart and wasn't sure for a moment if it was his heart or her own. And then she realised it was both their hearts, beating together as one.

He lifted the blanket away from her and slid the nightie from her shoulders. He swung his legs on to the bed, and then he was pulling her against him once more, and the rough sweater was a teasing delight against her bare skin. He began to kiss her, and her mouth opened willingly to his as she joyfully returned kiss for kiss. With one hand he moulded her against him, with the other he explored the soft curve of shoulders and the arch of her back, sliding down to her waist and her hips and her thighs.

There was no thought left in her, no shame or resistance. She did not even think of possible consequences as she pushed her hand under his sweater and began an exploration of her own. Bone and muscle were hard and angular beneath her fingers, and she was certain no man had ever been shaped quite like this. She felt him shudder at her touch, as if it stirred him very much, and for a moment her fingers halted. Then they moved once more. She wanted to know the feel of him, had to know, because she loved him so much.

Blye took his lips away from hers and began to kiss her breasts. As her nipples swelled and hardened Nicola was filled with an ache that she had not thought possible. Each of her senses was electrically alive. I love you, she said the words silently, I love you.

She felt as if she was drowning in a ride of sensuousness and love. There was nothing she could deny him. Not any more.

His hands were at his sweater, about to pull it over his head, when there was a knock at the door. They froze. 'I don't believe it! Not Mrs Barnes again, surely,' Blye whispered. 'Does she have a sixth sense?'

Another knock, and Nicola was glad the door was locked. Then someone called 'Nicola!' An impatient voice—Gloria.

Nicola was silent a moment. She looked at Blye and he nodded. She called back, 'Yes?'

'Can you open the damn door?'

'Not right now.'

She would go. Whatever Gloria wanted could wait.

'Do you know where Blye is?' Gloria called.

Blye winked and Nicola suppressed a giggle as she shouted back, 'Haven't a clue!'

'I've looked everywhere. Are you sure he isn't with you?'

'Quite sure. Perhaps he's in *your* bungalow, Gloria.' Nicola put a hand over her lips to suppress a fresh shudder of amusement. 'Why not go and look?'

There was a moment of silence, then Gloria said grumpily, 'Well, we're due to leave soon. He'll turn up, I suppose.'

Only when she'd obviously walked away did they feel free to talk. 'Well handled!' Blye was weak with laughter. 'You're not as innocent as you seem. Perhaps you're putting me on after all.'

'You'll have to find that out for yourself.' Nicola slanted him a mock demure smile.

'I'll have great pleasure doing just that.' A tongue flicked out and tickled a small earlobe. 'Unfortunately it's a pleasure that will have to wait.'

'Really?'

'Really, you wanton girl. Gloria just reminded me that duty is about to call—on us both. Get dressed, Nicola. I'll try to slip out of here unseen—meet you at the bus!'

Nicola glanced at the mirror before leaving the bungalow. Wanton, Blye had called her. There was a sheen in her eyes, a glow on her cheeks. Was this the look of wantonness? She grinned suddenly at her reflection, her teeth small and white against her apricot tan. She had never felt happier. Certainly she had never felt quite so vital and feminine as she did today.

'A pleasure that will have to wait,' Blye had said in parting. The words suggested that there would be a next time. Nicola gave a small sigh of happiness as she turned to the door and closed it behind her.

Blye was already at the bus when she reached it. He did not say anything as she boarded, but the eyes that met hers seemed to hold a look that was only for her, and she felt a new surge of happiness. Even Gloria's carping—and the suggestion that the tour-guide should not have been the last one to arrive—did nothing to mar the way she felt.

Euphoria seemed to lift her above petty irritations. For some reason Gloria was ruder than ever. Nicola smiled and fended the hostility with casual grace. 'Well done!' Blye whispered once, and Nicola marvelled that he did not realise that for once Gloria did not worry her.

The early-morning trip over, they returned to camp for breakfast. The jays were everywhere. The little birds, their plumage a deep jewel-blue, hopped on to tables and pecked crumbs from plates left standing unattended. Cheeky and unafraid, they were a constant source of amusement for the guests.

One found some crumbs on Gloria's plate. 'Blye, look!' she called. 'Oh, I must record this for posterity. Nicola, will you take a picture of us with the birds?'

In her euphoric state Nicola did not mind even this. Blye came to stand beside Gloria, who put her arm around his waist and smiled coyly into his face. It was an unlikely picture—the sophisticated Gloria with the little birds that gave amusement to lesser mortals than herself—but if the woman wanted a memento of the occasion that was her business. At any other time Nicola might have suffered a pang at the intimacy of the scene. Today, it seemed, nothing could shake her.

CHAPTER EIGHT

WHEN the bus set out again after breakfast, it was as if the animals sensed Nicola's exultant mood and wanted to be seen.

Almost from the moment they left camp there was game. A water-tower stood outside the gate, and monkeys gambolled up and down it, swinging from girders, leaping hither and thither to catch one another's tails. Just a few yards beyond it stood a giraffe, long neck bending gracefully to the leaves of a maroela tree. Blye stopped the bus long enough for the passengers to take all the pictures they wanted.

There were times when the tour had gone an hour or more without seeing anything more interesting than a solitary impala or a bird that rose from an acaccia at sight of the bus. Nicola had learned that an animal near the road can usually be seen easily: if it is camouflaged or hidden in the bush only an alert eye will spot it. But often the animals are very far from the road and so much of the game is unobserved.

Today was special. Every few minutes there was fresh cause for photos. They had been on the road almost an hour when Blye made a sign to Nicola. Puzzled, she followed his pointing finger. For a moment she saw nothing more than bush and a distant anthill. And then the anthill moved, took shape.

A lion! Excitement coursed through Nicola. Novice tour-guide that she was, she had never seen a lion roaming free. For a few moments she forgot her official capacity. She was just a visitor to the game park, and she was seeing the king of beasts, and she thought she would choke on the thrill of it.

It was almost a minute before she recovered herself. 'A lion!' she announced then on a note of elation. In moments the bus was a buzz of noise, a mass of craning necks. It was the one animal every person had dreamed of seeing.

Nicola turned to Blye. 'Thank you.'

He grinned. 'I didn't conjure him up.'

'You could have pointed him out. You let me do it.'

'You'd have seen him a moment later anyway. Enjoy the king, Nicola.'

His eyes were warm, and his smile reached straight to her heart. There was no mockery in it, none of the hardness Nicola had seen so often. There was only amusement, and the tenderness which she had glimpsed in the bungalow such a short while ago.

She longed to touch him, to bury her fingers in his hair once more, to trace the shape of his lips and his eyes. She kept her hands very firmly at her sides. But as she turned to look at the lion she thought she would burst with happiness.

There was a hush in the bus as the lion began to move towards the road. It emerged from the scrub and every line was sharp and well defined. A fully-grown male—there was the mane and the swinging tail, the proud, powerful walk.

Not for nothing was the lion called the king of the jungle, Nicola thought. No other animal could equal it for power and dignity and a bearing that was both regal and arrogant.

Involuntarily she glanced at Blye. Once before she had compared him to a lion. Both were powerful, arrogant, overwhelmingly male. Unmatched—surely.

A new buzz of excitement had her swinging back to the window. The lion had come closer. Suddenly through the bush—camouflaged until this moment—came more lions, another male, and two females, and then four frolicking cubs. The cubs rolled on their backs in the scrub, legs in the air; they looked like happy kittens.

The click-click of cameras was a steady sound and from the back of the bus, above the excitement, someone shouted, 'I go back to the States a happy man!'

Laughter greeted Jim Slade's remark. It was laughter that had in it a sense of sharing. Each of the passengers had hoped to see at least one lion, but Nicola had explained at the beginning of the trip that lions are rarely seen. Lazy animals, they are content to lie in the long grass, getting up only when it suits them.

'Thank you, my dear,' Mrs Barnes said to Nicola. 'I'll never forget this.'

Nicola looked at Blye. He was watching her. They exchanged a smile, a special smile somehow, and for a long moment it seemed to her that they were quite alone in the bus.

The lions reached the road and looked at the bus without shyness or fear. There was a crazy clicking of cameras as the cubs gambolled. And then the lions pushed through the bush on the other side of the road. Within moments there was not even a sign of them in the underbrush.

Blye started up the bus once more as Nicola said, 'Now you can understand why it's so important not to put a foot out of a vehicle. You might think there wasn't an animal in miles and all the while a lion could be lying in the grass. The bush is incredibly deceptive.'

There was silence as the passengers digested her words. Then Gloria said in the bored voice that Nicola found so riling, 'Doesn't our little guide sound just like a schoolmarm? What she doesn't realise is that we're adults, not a bunch of silly kids.'

Had she been talking down to the group? Nicola felt her cheeks grow warm. As her head turned in Blye's direction she heard Derek say, 'For heaven's sake, Gloria, give Nicola a break!'

Blye's face showed no expression. Only in his eyes did she see something, the merest flicker. Nicola was reminded of the day when he'd warned her to be careful with Gloria. Perhaps he had been wise to say nothing. Yet she could not help wishing that Blye, not Derek, had spoken out on her behalf. And now she was being unfair, unfair to Derek, Nicola thought, and wondered why sometimes nothing made very much sense.

A little of the joy seemed to have gone out of the day. And that made even less sense. She would *not* let Gloria's pettiness mar her happiness. Soon they would be at the hippo pool, and she would have other things to think about.

Fifty yards from the hippo pool the passengers dismounted. At the foot of a hilly path stood a guard, rifle in hand. There was no fence around the area and its surroundings. It was one of the very few places other than a camp where people were allowed to be out of a vehicle.

As they took the path to the river, Mrs Barnes asked, 'Is it safe?'

'Oh yes.'

'I was thinking of the lions. . . .'

Nicola had been thinking of them too. It was less than half an hour since they had been seen. How could anyone be sure that there would be no lions in the immediate vicinity of the pool?

'It's safe here,' said Blye before she could speak. His voice was reassuring. 'For some reason predators never come to this spot. That's why we can walk here.'

'Well, if you're sure. . . .'

'As sure as I can be.'

Nicola wondered if the elderly woman felt as safe with Blye as she herself did. Silly to believe that no harm could come to her in his presence, yet some instinct made her believe just that.

'The guard has a gun,' Mrs Barnes said anxiously.

'More of a token than anything else,' Blye told her, but Nicola knew that in the unlikely eventuality of a dangerous animal appearing the guard would have no hesitating in shooting. Not that anything would happen.

The same concern had been voiced during the training session, and Nicola remembered the instructor's reply. 'There are men who have lived in these parts many years, and they know the ways and the habits of the big game. They know where it's safe to walk, and when. Delayney Tours would never take risks with people's lives.'

The viewpoint was at the top of a rugged pile of rock. Nicola helped Mrs Barnes up, the others made their own way.

They looked down on to the river and found that the sun was shining on the water, splintering it into a thousand diamonds. Beneath the rocks, where the river widened into a pool, were the hippos—a whole school of them, lazy, slumbering, huge jaws opening now and then for air in a boiling mass of bubbles and foam. As always the cameras were busy.

Nicola was not as excited by the hippos as the rest of the group. There were other things on her mind—the excitement of seeing the lions, the small incident with Gloria.

The wonderful moments with Blye. Though there could be no future with Blye, she loved him. No matter that their lives would take them along different paths—and they must be different, the very nature of their worlds dictated it—she knew that he would always occupy a special place in her heart. There had been a time when she had wondered if what she felt was just sexual attraction. Sex was a part of it, she knew that now, it was a stronger force then she had ever dreamed possible. But above all she was filled with the love of a woman for a man, a love that was deep and abiding.

That being the case, Blye's lovemaking that morning was a memory she would always cherish. She had come so close to surrendering herself totally to him. If Gloria had not called when she did, she would have done so. Would she have regretted the act later? Perhaps, for there would have been the knowledge that she had experienced something that she would never know again. But there would also have been fulfilment, an even more precious memory to store in her mind against the inevitable loneliness that lay ahead.

While the group took photos, Nicola climbed a little higher. A wind had risen, it played in her hair and cooled her cheeks. It drowned out the sound of talking, so that Nicola felt that she could have been quite alone in the world. All around her stretched the bushveld, an endless vista of scrub and thorny bushes, of rocks and trees. It was a picture that had existed for centuries. It was Africa, before the advent of cities.

Exhilarated, Nicola lifted her face to the wind. She had no fear of lions in this spot, yet there was a thrill in the knowledge that they were out there, somewhere, not more than a few miles from here. She had seen them, would perhaps see them again. The veld was still, silent except for the wind. Nothing stirred. A deceptive stillness, for in the bush was game, invisible, but there all the same. Nicola knew that this spot would become one of her favourites. She would come here often as a tour-guide, and while her group watched the hippos she would think of Blye.

On these rocks she could forget his place in the high-powered world of business. In her memory he would always be a part of the vastness of veld and sky that she saw all around her. Here, she felt, was where he really belonged.

A sudden scream. Appalled, Nicola looked down the slope. Maria Mavroni screamed again. Below her, at the foot of a crevice, lay a still form. Nicola guessed it was Anton, the young husband.

In moments she had rejoined the group. 'What happened?' she demanded of Blye.

'Anton wanted a better angle for a picture— tried to jump across the crevice. Get that girl under control, Nicola, she's hysterical. I'm going down.'

'Blye. . . .' she began, and broke off. Don't go, she'd wanted to say. Don't put yourself in jeopardy. But he had to help, she knew that. 'Be careful,' was all she said as she touched his arm.

She was going to Maria when she saw Gloria. The woman had been watching her, had heard her brief plea, had seen her touch Blye's arm. Such a small gesture, but it seemed to have enraged Gloria, for her face was hard, her expression as hostile as Nicola had seen it.

Briefly their eyes met, held. There was no softening on Gloria's face, no smile, not the smallest hint of understanding for the urgency of the moment. She was totally self-centred, Nicola realised, and wondered how Blye could have let himself become involved with her.

Forget Gloria. There were things to be done. If Gloria was a menace to Nicola's peace of mind, she was also utterly unimportant.

Deliberately Nicola shifted her gaze. Putting an arm around Maria's shoulders, she spoke to her gently. 'Don't worry, Maria. We're taking care of things.' Meaningless words in a sense, for it was not known as yet if Anton was badly hurt. But necessary, for Maria had to be calmed. Though the pretty young bride did not understand English, Nicola hoped that the tone of her words would get through to her and that she would be reassured.

Gradually Maria grew quieter. She was weeping, but the shuddering and the screams had stopped. 'I'll take over, dear. I think Blye needs you.' Nicola looked up and saw Mrs Barnes. Gratefully she let the older women look after Maria and knew that in her motherly care the girl would find comfort.

She went to the edge of the rocks where the rest of the group watched Blye's progress. He was at the bottom of the crevice and was bending over Anton's inert body. After a few moments he looked up. 'I'll need some help,' he called at length.

'I'm coming!' Nicola shouted down.

'I'll go,' Derek offered.

'No.' She was firm. 'I've learned some first-aid.'

'Nicola. . . .'

'It's my job, Derek.'

Good thing she had brought the first-aid kit with her, she thought as she turned away. When the instructor had stressed the importance of keeping it at hand always it had seemed an unnecessary precaution. She wondered now what would be needed.

'Nicola. . . .' Derek tried again to detain her, 'this is a man's job.'

'No such thing these days.' She smiled at him. 'I want to go, Derek. I'll be fine.'

'Anything to be with Blye,' she heard Gloria say, but she refused to look back.

As she clambered down over the rocks she saw the jump Anton had attempted. He must have known he was taking a chance. Why hadn't Maria stopped him?

Would she be able to stop Blye from doing what he wanted? Nicola wondered. Would she try? The question was futile, she realised a moment later, for it presupposed a relationship that went deeper than the very temporary association of a tour-guide and the man who drove her bus. Just for a moment, involuntarily, she had thought of herself as having a permanent place in Blye's life. As his wife! Heavens, was she really so foolish?

Blye watched her descent. He called to her a few times, pointing out footholds, and when she came within reach of him he stretched out his hand to her and helped her the rest of the way.

For a moment longer than necessary she kept her hand in his, and wondered if he noticed it. Then she became Nicola, tour-guide, and turned her attention to Anton.

He was lying quite still, and his face was very white. 'He's not . . . not dead?' Her voice shook.

'He's breathing and his pulse-rate is nothing to worry about.'

'Thank goodness for that!'

'He's knocked himself out, but I think he's starting to come round.'

'Badly hurt?' she asked.

'Bleeding in two places. Have to get them bandaged before we can move him. I'm glad you have the first-aid kit, Nicola.'

Blye must have learned first-aid himself, Nicola realised as she watched him, and wondered if there was anything he could not do. The sight of blood shocked her, but she was able to control her squeamishness. He told her what to do, and she complied. Once she looked up, and in that moment he looked up too.

'Good girl,' he murmured softly, then turned back to Anton.

They worked together well in the hot crevice with the sun blinding on the rock walls. A team, Nicola thought. There were many ways in which a man and a woman could be a team. Once more there came into her mind a picture of herself as Blye's wife. In the particular intimacy of the moment this picture was harder to push away.

Anton stirred suddenly. His eyes opened and

he looked at Nicola, his expression dazed. 'Maria?' he was puzzled—and then he gave a little moan of pain.

'You'll be all right,' said Nicola in the gentle voice she had used with his wife.

'Maria,' he said again.

'She's waiting at the top of the cliff.'

'He doesn't understand a word you say,' said Blye.

'I think he does.'

A dust-stained hand touched hers. 'Perhaps you're right.' A long thumb made one slow stroking movement. 'You're quite a girl.' The hand left hers. 'Time to get Anton up.'

'Will we manage?'

'Your swain seemed eager to help.' Blye grinned wickedly at the sight of her face. 'I'll shout up to Derek. He can come down now.'

'You're sure Anton's all right?' Nicola asked as Derek began his descent.

'Pretty sure.'

Nicola tried to imagine how she would feel were she in Maria's place, waiting at the top of the cliff, wondering if Blye was badly hurt. Praying.

'Maria will be relieved,' she said simply. 'Blye, Derek's not my swain.'

'I'm glad to hear it.'

She jerked around, heart leaping. 'You are?'

'He could never cope with you.'

Derek was coming down slowly, carefully. A pebble was disloged by a probing foot, and slithered suddenly down the rock-face. Derek paused and looked down, and Nicola heard him take a breath. Then he was moving again.

'Don't knock him, Blye.'

'I'm not knocking him. He couldn't cope with you all the same. Under that gentle exterior there's spirit and steel. Passion too. You need a strong man to match you.'

A strong man indeed. A very special man. A man like a lion. You, Blye. *I* know it, I wish *you* did.

'Good thing I've nobody in mind,' she said lightly. 'Look, Blye, Derek's almost down.'

It was no easy matter to carry Anton up the cliff-face. Once more Blye directed; Nicola and Derek followed what he said. Inch by painful inch they worked their way up the crevice. Anton, no longer unconscious, moaned a few times. He said a few words which Nicola did not understand, but she knew that he was indeed all right. For a while he would be bruised and stiff, but he had suffered no major injuries.

As they neared the top, eager hands reached for Anton, helping him over the edge. Nicola was relieved to see that he had recovered sufficiently to walk.

And then Maria had her arms around him. Through her tan her face was very pale, and she was crying. Shaken as Anton was, he tried to comfort her. The rest of the group turned away, letting the young couple have the moment of relief to themselves.

'Well done, Blye!' Gloria put her hand on his arm. 'Endangering your own life for an idiot who didn't deserve it.'

'Thank you, but Nicola and Derek are equally deserving of praise.'

'It's one of Nicola's duties to administer first-aid.' Gloria was unable to keep the anger from her voice.

Blye grinned at Nicola. 'She deserves as much credit as I do—if not more.'

Gloria must have caught a serious inflection in his tone, for she looked uncertain a moment. Then she smiled, the glorious smile she reserved solely for Blye. 'Of course, darling. There seems to be no end to young Nicola's qualities.'

'I'm only just discovering them myself.' Blye's eyes were on Nicola again. She saw him look at her lips, then his eyes moved down to her throat, her figure. It did not seem to worry him that Gloria observed him. Nicola trembled.

'And yet in some ways she's inexperienced,' Gloria persisted.

'Ah,' Blye intoned the one word very lazily. Nicola wondered if Gloria knew he was not referring to her tour-guiding abilities.

I'm out of my league, she thought. These people are rich and sophisticated. They play their games by different rules from the ones I'm used to. They talk another language.

'Who hired her?' The woman was openly curious.

Blye shrugged and winked at Nicola.

'Darling, this isn't my first safari. I've seen other guides. They're different.'

'Pehaps that's the very reason Nicola was chosen.'

'I don't understand. . . .'

'And I'm unable to explain. Please excuse me, Gloria, I want to have another look at Anton. Then, Nicola, I think we should all make tracks for the bus.'

As Nicola watched him walk away she felt a glow of satisfaction. So much of the conversation had been wrapped in hidden meanings, most of

which she had understood only too well. But this
was not the moment to dwell on them. There was
something else that stood out above all else.
Something that buoyed her spirits.

Blye had not discussed her with Gloria after
all. From what Mrs Barnes had told her, the
relationship between the two was close, painfully
close as far as Nicola was concerned. She had
been convinced that Gloria would have known
the circumstances in which she had been hired,
that Blye and Gloria would have laughed together
about her, the nãve and almost penniless girl
who had travelled so far to the offices of
Delayney Tours, in search of a job for which she
was in no way equipped.

But Gloria did *not* know. That much the last
few minutes had made clear. Blye had shielded
Nicola from his companion's scorn, and the fact
was absurdly important to her.

At a touch on her arm she looked down. Long
red nails, immaculately groomed, pricked her
skin. Repelled, Nicola managed to quell the
impulse to jerk her arm away. Slowly, giving
herself time to get her features under control, she
looked up at Gloria. 'Yes?' she queried politely.

'Drop the act,' Gloria snapped. 'Blye's not
around to see it.'

'I don't think I understand.'

'You're the simpering little innocent when he's
around—all radiance and youthful charm!'

'Suppose you get to the point, Mrs Payne.'
Those who knew Nicola well could have told
Gloria that when her voice was low, her words
slow and polite, she was very angry.

'The point is that you're so terribly obvious.
You virtually gobble Blye up with your eyes.'

Were her feelings really so apparent? Nicola felt a stab of pain deep inside her, and knew she must not let Gloria see how she felt. It was an effort to hold the woman's stare steadily, but somehow she managed.

'You're mistaken.' An icy politeness.

'Come off it, Nicola! You've been after Blye since the moment you saw him.'

Remember that I'm a tour-guide. That she's a member of this tour. That I'm duty bound to be polite to her. Don't let this awful woman see that I'd like to claw my fingers across those flawless cheeks.

'You really are mistaken, Mrs Payne. If you'll excuse me, I want to see the group back to the bus.'

'They're perfectly capable of getting there themselves. Don't you know that Blye has no time for innocent girls, Nicola? He despises them.'

'In that case I'm no competition for you, am I?' This time the words were out before she could stop them. Dimly Nicola remembered saying something very similar to Gloria once before.

The beautiful face took on an angry flush and the nails bit cruelly into the soft skin of Nicola's arm. 'You're not innocent at all,' Gloria hissed. 'You pretend to be unsophisticated, yet now that you know who Blye is—all that money—he's doubly attractive, isn't he?'

'Don't judge me by your own standards,' Nicola said blindly. 'And please let go of my arm, you're hurting me.'

'We'll get a few things clear first. Leave Blye alone!'

'That sounds like a threat.'

'It is, honey, it is. We both know that he was in your bungalow this morning.'

Nicola gaped at her. 'How do you know?' she stammered after a moment.

'He was nowhere else.' Gloria's eyes glittered, and Nicola knew that she had let herself be trapped. In the circumstances it was best not to attempt a denial. The other woman, well versed in these matters, would demolish her.

'You lured him in!' Gloria went on.

'I'm not in the habit of luring men,' Nicola said quietly.

She felt ill. All morning Blye's lovemaking had been on her mind. A golden memory, warming her, making her feel happier than she had ever been. Now, with just a few words, the memory that she had thought she would cherish all her life was being tainted, uglied.

'I have to go,' she said.

'You might as well know,' said Gloria, just as if she had not heard her, 'that these little encounters mean nothing to Blye. He's a hot-blooded man, he takes his fun where he can get it, and when it's over it's forgotten. It's the girl who gets hurt every time.'

Useless to protest that she had not slept with Blye. Gloria would not believe her.

'You've made it clear all along that you dislike me.' Anger was beginning to creep into Nicola's voice. 'Why should you care if I get hurt?'

'I don't give a damn. What I demand is that you keep away from Blye.'

Even Gloria had never been quite so outspoken. Nicola stared at her.

'He's mine!' the other woman hissed.

Could a man like Blye be owned? 'You're engaged to him?' Deep inside Nicola was weeping. If only she could end this conversation, get back to camp, seek the refuge of her bungalow where she could let the tears fall.

'Of course. My divorce was well aired, I've no doubt you know all about it. I've heard some of the others talking—Mrs Barnes. . . .'

'I don't want to hear this.'

The sharp nails bit deeper. 'You'll hear, honey. I got divorced because of Blye. I've sacrificed a lot for his sake. He belongs to me, and no little upstart is going to get in my way. Do you understand what I've said?'

I understand that you're an evil woman—icy, selfish, grasping. You're not worthy of Blye. But you'll get him all the same.

'I heard every word you said.' Aloofly Nicola shifted her eyes. With her free hand she removed Gloria's nails from her arm and without waiting to see if the woman followed her or not she walked to the bus.

CHAPTER NINE

THE euphoria was gone, with it the feelings of
warmth and happiness. Earlier Nicola had
thought that nothing could mar the beauty of this
day. As she joined the rest of the group she
wondered how she would get through the rest of
it. She did not let herself think to the end of the
tour. Just let me survive this day, she prayed.

Blye threw her a questioning look as she
boarded the bus. 'Feeling all right?' His tone was
low.

Pretending to make a note on her clipboard,
she averted her eyes. 'Fine.'

'You were a long time coming back.'

'Just making sure everyone was all right. Mrs
Barnes needs help.'

'She was back before you were. Nicola, look at
me.' And more firmly, when she did not respond,
'Look at me!'

Foolish to risk a scene when the group, Gloria
in particular, were interested spectators. As
calmly as possible she met his gaze.

His eyes were steady, his expression concerned.
It was an expression which wrenched at her
heart. His lips were slightly tilted in the
enquiring glance that had become so familiar, and
his jaw was a long firm line.

Nicola did not want to look at him. With every
moment she loved him more, and correspondingly
the inevitability of future heartbreak increased.
Despite herself, she could not stop herself

looking at him. As she could not seem to stop loving him.

A man above all other men. Gloria really was not worthy of him. She was hard and cold and scheming. She was also very beautiful. Was her beauty enough for Blye?

'What happened, Nicola?'

She was not given to tale-telling. Besides, he would take Gloria's side every time. If Blye was the cause of Gloria's divorce, then their relationship was deep indeed.

'Nothing happened.' She marvelled that she could make herself sound so casual.

'Nicola.'

The group had taken their seats by this time. Cameras were at the ready. There were restless stirrings, a few coughs.

'Leave it at that, Blye.' She forced a light smile. 'It's very hot—we should get going.'

He studied her a moment longer, then he shrugged and turned the key in the ignition.

Not content with her victory—for in changing Nicola's mood she had indeed scored a victory—Gloria continued her carping all day. She found fault with everything. The seat by her window was dusty. The steak at lunch-time was tough. The road they travelled had few animals. The fault-finding never ended, and each time the blame lay with Nicola.

It was true that the afternoon drive yielded little in the way of game. Nicola's nerves, already jagged from the morning's encounter with Gloria, felt raw. The other woman's shout rang out suddenly. 'Something! Stop the bus!'

'Where?' People craned their heads, searching the bush.

'Behind the fever trees.' She sounded more excited than Nicola had heard her. 'Some kind of buck, a big one!'

As if on cue, the animal's body emerged a little way through the trees.

'A sable antelope! Isn't it stunning!' Gloria enthused.

The animal changed position. A white line circled its rump.

'How's that for a sable? Why didn't you spot it, Nicola? What else have you missed?'

It was one barb too many. Blandly Nicola said, 'That antelope, Gloria, is a waterbuck.'

'Rubbish! I know a sable antelope when I see one.' Gloria's excitement had turned to anger.

Sable antelope, waterbuck—all the same family. Later Nicola would wonder why the issue was so important. She heard Blye say softly, 'Nicola,' but she did not heed him. Gloria had caught her on the raw once too often today. This was one instance where she would not get away with it.

'It's a waterbuck. Surely you couldn't have missed the white circle around its rear end?'

A hush had fallen over the group. The tension between Gloria and Nicola filled the bus.

'Blye,' Gloria appealed, 'tell Nicola she's wrong.'

Don't, Blye, please. Nicola sent out a small silent prayer. Don't let this woman belittle me again. I've had as much as I can take.

'We have a book back at the camp,' she said aloud before Blye could speak. 'You'll be able to satisfy yourself that this is a waterbuck.'

Silence. In the stationary bus the heat was intense. Gloria said again, 'Blye.'

'It's very hot.' He spoke for the first time and his manner was short. 'I suggest we go on.'

He was on her side! Nicola was exultant. Without actually putting the fact into words he had indicated to Gloria that she was wrong. Gloria's cheeks were flushed with anger and her lips were tightly set. Nicola felt that in a small way she had triumphed over the woman who had set out so deliberately to humiliate her.

The sense of triumph lasted through the drive back to camp, through the braaivleis that followed. When they had eaten Derek initiated a sing-song. Blye did not fetch his guitar, but Derek's enthusiasm was sufficient to engender a relaxed mood around the fire. Nicola joined in lustily with the rest. She felt elated, vindicated.

'That was some point you scored over the dragon,' Derek said to her quietly between songs.

Nicola shook her head, refusing to rise to the remark. But she smiled. She felt so good that it did not seem to matter that Blye did not join in the singing, that Gloria was still tight-lipped. It did not even matter when they left the fire and walked away through the darkness. Nothing mattered tonight.

She was still smiling as she said goodnight to the group. She was getting ready for bed when she heard a knock. In her nightdress she opened the door.

'Blye!' The name came out on a burst of pleasure.

'Nicola.' His own tone was hard.

She stared at him as he walked past her into the room. His eyes were unreadable in the dim light, but his jaw had never looked quite so grim.

'What are you doing here?'

But even before he spoke she knew the answer.

'You're going to apologise to Gloria.'

'No!'

'Now.' One word. Authoritative.

'I will not!'

'Yes, Nicola, you will. You will come with me now.'

He was so certain of himself, so utterly confident that she would do his bidding. He was not Blye now, the Blye Peterson with whom she had fallen crazily in love. He was Beldon Delayney, head of a great world of business—a tycoon, a man whom people hastened to obey. Did it occur to him that someone would not? And a small insignificant girl, a mere tour-guide, at that?

She lifted her chin proudly. 'You're wasting your time.'

He looked at her for a moment without speaking. His face was a study in distaste, Nicola thought, as if she were some insect that he found particularly repellent.

'I don't have to tell you that you were very rude,' he said coldly.

Any point arguing? Probably not, but nothing lost in trying.

'You're talking about what happened this afternoon.'

'Quite.'

'I merely explained that Gloria's sable antelope was a waterbuck.'

'You took great pleasure in doing so.'

She grinned at him. 'That's beside the point.'

She should have been prepared for the hand that caught her wrist, twisting her around against him. There was nothing remotely lover-like in the gesture, nevertheless it did not stop the response that flared through her body every time he touched her.

'Gloria is very upset,' he went on.

Do her feelings mean so much to you? Oh, Blye, Blye, why did I have to fall in love with you?

'What about my feelings?' she asked quietly. 'Don't they count?'

Lowly creatures don't have feelings. Don't you know that, Nicola?

His other hand went to her arm. The fingers were firm on her skin, in the very spot where Gloria's had been earlier that day, but the feel of them was so different. Almost like a caress, though in the circumstances it couldn't be that.

'Your feelings count.' His voice was rough. 'You should know that, Nicola.'

'Well, then?'

'You are a tour-guide. Gloria is a member of your group.'

'The customer is always right,' she said dully.

'Something like that. Come with me, Nicola.'

'I won't!' Anger seared her. 'Why don't you tell the truth, Blye? You're so concerned about Gloria because she's your mistress.'

Deny it. Please deny it. I may not believe you, but just to hear you deny it might give me some comfort.

She thought she heard a hiss of indrawn breath. She stopped breathing herself while she waited for his reply. Then, in a voice that was totally devoid of expression, Blye said, 'My relationship with Gloria has nothing to do with the issue.' Not for the first time today she felt sick. 'My concern is for Gloria as a member of the group, as a paying customer of Delayney Tours. Come along, Nicola, she's waiting.'

'She'll wait a long time. I will not apologise to that woman!'

The ball was back in his court. He would not accept what she said, she knew that. But what would be his next step?

He pulled her against him. The hand that had gripped her wrist went to her back, moved over it with a sensuousness that was quite deliberate. Nicola shuddered. Blye knew his power over her, knew how to reach her. She hated him for what he was doing, and hoped that her awakening body would not betray her.

'No, Blye.' She tried to move away from him, and found that his strength was greater than her own.

His sweater was rough against her cheek, and the tongue that played around an ear-lobe was a sweet torture. 'We were interrupted this morning. Remember?' He had brought his mouth down now, his lips were just inches from hers as he spoke.

'I remember,' she said bumpily.

'We agreed to return to it. It's what we both want, Nicola.'

It was what she wanted. Useless to deny it. Blye must feel the shuddering warmth of her body. Expert with women that he was, he would know just how much he had aroused her.

'Apologise to Gloria and then we'll come back here.'

'No!' This time her anger was such that she was able to pull away from him. How dared he try to get around her this way! It was unforgivable.

'Get out, Blye!' she snapped.

'We'll go together.'

'Never!'

He looked down at her. The hardness was back in his face. There was also something else—not quite a tenderness, not quite a question. Nicola wished she could define what she saw, and wondered if her heartbeats were audible in the tiny room.

'You do know that you were rude?' Blye insisted.

'I could have been more understanding.' It was as much as she was prepared to concede.

'You wouldn't have pressed the point with someone else. Mrs Barnes or Mary Slade.'

'Perhaps not.'

'You dislike Gloria.'

'She's given me little reason to like her. This morning, at the hippo pool. . . .' She stopped and looked away.

'Something happened, I know that. I gave you the chance to explain.' He sounded impatient.

'Right, you did. What about the rest of the day, Blye? On and on with her sarcasm, her innuendoes. Didn't you hear her?'

'I heard. You still miss the point. You are a tour-guide. . . .'

'And Gloria is an esteemed guest,' she cut in, her voice high.

'Correct. There will always be people who will annoy you, Nicola.'

'There's only one Gloria Payne!'

'And if you're going to keep your job,' he continued, as if he had not heard her, 'you're going to have to learn to treat such people with tact.'

She drew breath. 'Are you firing me, Blye?'

'That rather depends on you, my dear.'

For a long moment they stood looking at each other. He had never looked more ruthless, Nicola thought. The deepset eyes were relentless, the lips very firm, the long line of the jaw had a hint of cruelty. And he had never looked quite so handsome. Sexual attractiveness was a part of him that he wore as easily as an old sweater.

I'm crazy, Nicola thought. The battle lines have been drawn. Blye is my adversary. And all I can think of is how I long to be in his arms.

She curled her nails hard into the palms of her hands. 'I will not apologise.'

'That's your final word?'

'Absolutely.'

'I see.' He smiled, a lazy smile that made her feel infinitely uneasy. His eyes moved deliberately to lips that quivered despite her effort to control them, to her throat and then down to breasts that he had caressed that morning. When he looked up again he was still smiling. 'I see,' he said again. 'Well, Nicola, now you have only yourself to blame for the consequences.'

She was trembling. 'What consequences?'

'You will not be coming with us tomorrow.'

He couldn't mean it. Even Blye could not subject her to such humiliation.

She found her voice. 'You can't do this to me!'

'Yes, my dear, I can.'

He turned. Before she understood what he meant to do he had scooped one safari suit from the chair where it lay, had taken the other two from their hangers.

'No, Blye!' She ran to him, tried to drag her clothes from his arm. 'Oh, Blye, no!'

He shrugged her off easily.

'Those are my clothes!'

'Apologise to Gloria and you'll have them back.'

'I can't do that.'

'Then you'll stay in this room till the end of the trip.'

He strode to the door and opened it. Carrying her clothes, every stitch that she possessed apart from her nightdress, he walked out into the night. She heard him say, 'Sleep well, Nicola.'

Outraged, she watched the door close behind him. Not even when Jonathan had broken off their engagement had she felt quite so humiliated—humiliated and terribly angry.

Owner of Delayney Tours Blye might be, lord of all he surveyed, but that did not give him the right to treat her in this fashion. 'I hate you, Blye,' she said into the silent room.

The lovely morning, when she had felt more alive and feminine and desirable than ever before in her life, seemed to have existed in another time, another world.

Stop thinking about Blye, about Gloria. Think what to do, how to get out of this fix.

A sudden hope entered her mind. Blye had been joking, surely. He was not a cruel man, there had been times when she had seen such warmth in his eyes, tenderness.

He must love Gloria deeply to behave so audaciously on her behalf, but he liked Nicola. Had liked her. Or had she only imagined the good times, the moments when there had been a golden rapport that she had thought she would cherish always? He had kissed her, had roused her to the heights, had seemed roused himself.

He must have felt some affection for her then—or had his behaviour merely stemmed from an insatiable need to conquer every woman in sight? The thought brought a pain that she tried to banish. She had enough to think about at this moment without trying to analyse Blye's motives for making love to her.

The minutes passed and still she stared at the door, willing it to open. Blye would come back. He *must*.

She did not know how long it took for the realisation to sink in that Blye would not come. That he had not been joking. Or if he had been the joke was on her.

Turning from the door, she felt weak. She sank on to her bed and buried her face in her pillow. Was this what her dreams had come to? she wondered as the first tears came. The end of a love that had been hopeless from the start. The end of a job for which she had sacrificed so much. Sent home in disgrace in a nightdress. It was not to be borne.

Suddenly she sat up. Was this what had become of her? Nicola Sloane weeping tears of self-pity into her pillow? Stripped of much that she held dear she might be, but even Blye could not strip her of her fighting spirit—unless she allowed him to.

Fiercely she dashed the tears from her eyes and cheeks and ran a hand through damp hair. There must be something she could do, some way she could fight back. Even if it meant fighting dirty.

Think, Nicola. Think carefully. Shut Blye from your mind, pretend you never loved him. Find a way out of this dilemma.

What were her options? She could apologise to

Gloria. Blye would return her clothes, and the tour would draw to a close with none of the group aware of what had happened.

It was the easy way out. It was also not an option. Fighting spirit to the fore now, Nicola was more than ever determined that she would not apologise.

She could appear the next morning in her nightdress. It would not take the group long to learn what had happened. Would their sympathies be with Gloria, the passenger who had been insulted by the tour-guide? Perhaps not. The woman was not well liked. There was a strong possibility that the sympathy of the group would be with Nicola. The joke would have rebounded on Blye.

Splendid!

Perhaps—not so splendid. As an employee of Delayney Tours—or was she already an ex-employee?—she would be wrong to behave in a manner that would give the company a bad name. She would also be humiliating Blye. It was what he deserved, but oddly the prospect lacked appeal.

Derek—he came to mind all at once. Perhaps he could help her. That he would be sympathetic to her cause, Nicola knew. If there was a way to sneak her clothes away from Blye, Derek would be the one to help her do it. She would appear at the bus the next morning, smartly dressd and ready for work, and the joke would be on Blye after all.

It was the solution she had been looking for. In an instant she was off the bed and making for the door.

She emerged from the bungalow to find the

night air chill on her skin. All she had on was her thin nightdress. Even her feet were bare, for Blye had taken her shoes along with her clothes. She shivered, and wrapped her arms around herself for warmth.

As she began to make her way in the direction of Derek's bungalow she speculated on Blye's whereabouts. Was he in his room, congratulating himself on the way he had handled the situation? Or was he with Gloria, telling her what had happened, promising her that an apology would yet be wrung from the recalcitrant Nicola?

Pain stirred within her at the thought of the two together, alone in the small bungalow. How long, she wondered, would she be tortured with thoughts of Blye? If only she could stop herself thinking about him.

The shortest way to Derek's bungalow led past the camp fence. Noises sounded through the bush, the calls and scufflings of unseen animals. A maniacal shriek rang through the night, and Nicola froze. The shriek came again, and she recognised it as a hyena's laugh. Nothing to be frightened of, for the beast could be miles from this spot, yet she was uneasy as she walked further.

The shape materialised quite suddenly. Nicola gave a scream of fright, then stepped weakly backwards as she realised that the shape was human.

'Not a good idea to walk here at this hour,' drily remarked a voice that was all too familiar.

'My stars, Blye, you frightened me!' she gasped.

'If I've frightened you into abandoning midnight strolls in the altogether then I'll have accomplished something.'

'I'm not in the altogether,' she snapped, fright giving way to anger.

'Very nearly.'

'Whose fault is that? You decided to take my clothes!'

'Which fact you couldn't wait to tell dear Derek.'

She gasped. 'How did you know?'

'There's not much I don't know about you, Nicola.' His tone was surprisingly seductive. 'Surely you realise that by now?'

She decided to ignore the comment. Voice cool, she said, 'Goodnight, Blye.'

He detained her as she made to go past him. 'You're going nowhere.'

'You can't stop me.'

'Can't I?' he drawled.

She felt enormously excited and despised herself for it. 'You may be my boss, Blye, but there are limits to your power.'

For answer he drew her to him. 'You're so cold, Nicola.'

Did he not feel the fires running through her? she wondered, and said aloud, 'The sooner I get to Derek the sooner I'll be warm.'

'What did you hope to elicit from him? His sympathy or his help?'

Tilting back her head, she stared up at him in the darkness, and wished she could read his face. 'You were waiting for me,' she said slowly.

'Come along, Nicola.' His voice was soft.

'It's no coincidence that you were out here.'

'You're getting very cold.'

'And very angry. Stop telling me what I can and can't do!'

He laughed, a low husky sound that fanned her

face and unnerved her. 'If talking is not what you like, then I won't talk.'

There was no escaping him as he scooped her off the ground, one arm at her back, the other supporting her knees. 'Nicola, sexy and stubborn. What am I going to do with you?'

Go on holding me just like this. Never put me down. Take me with you wherever you go. Love me.

'I hate you, Blye,' she said, when he'd dropped her to the ground in her bungalow.

'Do you?'

She should have been able to move away, but her limbs felt lethargic, as if they had no will of their own.

One arm was still around her. The other hand went to her shoulder, slid beneath the top of the nightdress to move silkily over bare skin. At the same time his mouth came down and his lips began a slow tantalising trail over her throat and her face, hovering near her lips, playing at the corners, deliberately heightening her mounting suspense by never staying in one spot for more than a moment.

'Is this what you wanted Derek to do with you?' he asked once.

'Yes,' she lied. 'Why ask questions when you know all the answers?' It was very hard to keep her voice cool.

'You're a provoking baggage that revenge is sweet sometimes.'

'I provoke you?' She danced him an innocent glance.

'You know darn well that you do. To distraction. Going to Derek would have been just one more instance. Don't you realise the stir it'd have caused when the rest of the group got to hear of it?'

'It would have been worth it,' she declared.

'You're utterly unscrupulous, Nicola. That's why I waylaid you.'

'I had to try, Blye.' She was appalled at the sob in her voice.

'And afterwards—assuming you'd have succeeded—would you have rewarded Derek by letting him make love to you?'

He would not have been allowed to lay one finger on me. I have the most awful feeling that you've spoiled me as far as other men are concerned. That I would be repelled if anyone else tried to kiss me.

'He'd have deserved the reward,' she said saucily.

'You'd have let him kiss you like this?'

His lips closed on hers again, hungrily this time, deeply, demanding a response and receiving it. There was no thought of resistance. She loved Blye, even now, when she'd told herself that she hated him.

He lifted his head. 'Would you, Nicola?'

'Yes.'

'And like this?' He was a little rough now.

With one movement he had pushed the nightdress from her shoulders, and then his lips were on her breast, kissing nipples that were swollen and hard.

'Well, Nicola?'

'Yes!' The word emerged raggedly this time, and she knew that she was saying yes to far more than his question. She wondered if he knew it too.

'And what would *you* have done?' he asked harshly.

'This.'

Fulfilling a deep need, she slid her hands beneath his sweater and pressed them flat against her chest, then let her fingers explore an angular hardness that extended to his shoulders. Involuntarily she arched her body against him.

He drew a deep shuddering breath. Then he said, 'My darling, Nicola, are you just a tease?'

'What do you think, Blye?'

He pushed her a little away from him. 'I think perhaps you really aren't as innocent as you pretend. Perhaps Gloria is right about that.'

So they *had* discussed her. The joy went out of the lovemaking. 'I want my clothes, Blye,' she pleaded.

'You know the terms.'

'I can't apologise.'

'Then it's stalemate.'

She was silent a moment before saying, 'The group will want to know where I am.'

'I'll tell them you're ill.'

He would do just that, and without batting an eyelid.

'They might want to visit me.'

'Your bungalow is off limits. One last thing before I go—don't try running to Derek. It won't work, Nicola.'

He was at the door when she asked, 'How long do you propose to keep me prisoner in here?'

He turned, his expression inscrutable. 'Until you apologise, or until the tour ends, whichever is the sooner.'

The door closed and Nicola crept beneath the sheets. This time, she was certain, Blye would not be back.

CHAPTER TEN

NICOLA woke early. Her head felt heavy and her eyes burned. The room was opaque with the light of dawn. Sitting up, she surveyed the room. Emptiness was its most striking quality. The only chair was bare of the uniform that had been draped over its back last night. In the small cupboard, the hangers were bare too.

In the moments before she had opened her eyes there had been the hope that she would see her uniforms. Blye would have relented. He'd have come into her bungalow while she was sleeping, would have put back her clothes. Last night he had intended merely to frighten her.

The empty room revealed the hollowness of her hopes. Blye's behaviour had not been a bluff.

She got out of bed and went to the window. The camp-grounds were quiet. There was no sign of life. But soon people would be waking, would dress and make for the bus. Nicola curled cold bare toes and swore, 'Damn you, Blye!'

'Temper hasn't improved with the night,' a cheerful voice remarked.

She spun round. Blye stood in the doorway, looking smart in a safari suit that was open at the neck and showed his tanned arms and legs to their best advantage.

The hope had not been hollow after all!

She went to him gladly. 'Oh, Blye, you've come! And you've brought my clothes.'

An eyebrow lifted. 'I have them with me.'

'Wretch! The ordeal you put me through!' She gave a laugh of relief. 'Let me have them. I should have known you'd come.'

'The terms haven't changed, Nicola.' His voice was curiously flat.

'Blye?'

He was looking at her, his eyes narrowed, unreadable. It was a moment or two before he said, 'You should have known that too.'

'I thought ... by now. ...' She stopped. 'Don't you understand what you're asking of me?'

A flicker in the dark eyes. 'I understand.'

'Well then. ...'

'I also understand what you did. Gloria's views haven't changed.'

Her relief, so exquisite and so short-lived, gave way to despair. 'Doesn't she have a sense of humour?' she sighed.

'She didn't find the situation amusing,' Blye said drily.

'She's an awful woman—arrogant, opinionated.'

'I'm not here to discuss Gloria's personality.'

'How can you tie yourself to that woman?' She had not meant to ask the question. But the words were out, there was no point in stopping. 'She's all wrong for you, Blye.'

'Are you going to apologise?' he wanted to know, ignoring her question.

She could feel tears gathering. She could not cry. *Would* not!

Blinking, she said fiercely, 'I was mistaken. You fit together beautifully. You're as arrogant and as horrible as she is!'

'Are you going to apologise?' His voice was

bland, as if nothing she said mattered to him.

'You know the answer.' She turned away.

'And you know the consequences.'

Her clothes were still in his arms when he left the bungalow.

She heard the voices of the group—Derek and Mrs Barnes, Jim Slade talking to May, and Anton shouting to Maria from the fence, obviously excited at something he had spotted. She heard Blye's laugh, deep and clear upon the still air, as casual as if nothing had happened that day to mar his peace of mind. Nicola clenched her fists and wished she had something to pound them on.

Presently the grounds grew quiet. Standing by the window, Nicola saw a bird far above her, a vulture, soaring and making a turn—solitary, yet free, to go where it wanted.

It was going to be a long, lonely day.

At midday there was a knock. Face carefully expressionless, Nicola went to the door. Nonplussed, she stared at the man who stood on the sun-baked step. Not Blye at all, but Derek.

'Nicola, how are you?' he asked.

' . . . Fine.'

'Blye said you were ill.'

The solution to the problem had come walking up to her doorway. Nicola took a breath. 'Come inside.'

Derek's eyes were on her body, a male look that took in the feminine curves beneath the thin fabric of her nightdress. Not an offensive look, however; nothing in it to make her sensuously aware of herself as a woman. Perhaps only Blye could have that effect on her.

'You spent the day in bed?' he asked.

'No.'

'Blye said. . . . And you're in your nightie.'

'It's all I possess right now,' Nicola said grimly. 'Derek, you have to help me.' In a few words she told him what had happened.

'You want me to steal your clothes back for you?'

'If you can.'

'Nothing to it.' Derek squared his shoulders. 'Blye doesn't scare me.'

'Oh, Derek, thanks!'

'Nothing to thank me for. The man's unique—arrogant as they come.'

'He's certainly unique,' Nicola murmured.

'He's just the driver, not your boss. Why do you let him do it to you?'

For a moment she was tempted to tell Derek the truth about Blye. She opened her mouth, then thought better of it. Blye had his reasons for travelling incognito, and would not take easily to Nicola disclosing his identity to a member of the group. She owed him nothing, she told herself fiercely. But Blye in an angry mood was a hard man to deal with. No need to add to her problems.

She gave a laugh that was more like a sob. 'Blye does pretty much what he wants. You will help me, Derek?'

'You bet!' His eyes had gone back to her body. 'Blye saw you like this?'

'Yes.'

'I'd like to kill him,' the young man muttered with sudden feeling. 'You're so lovely, Nicola—defenceless against a man like that.' In two quick steps he had closed the gap between them and had put his arms around her. 'You'll go on seeing me after the tour?'

'Derek. . . .'

He did not register her protest as he bent his head to kiss her. The kiss started tentatively but turned quickly to eager passion. I feel nothing, Nicola thought with despair.

She tried to push him away and felt his arms tighten. When he lifted his head for breath she said anxiously, 'Blye might come.'

'I'm not frightened of Blye Peterson.' In the tiny room Derek's voice was unnecessarily loud. 'Let him come and I'll make him sorry!'

'You will?' a lazy voice drawled.

They had not heard him come in. Derek's arms loosened just a little. Nicola was suddenly very aware of her barely clothed state. Looking into mocking eyes set deep in a rugged face, she felt her stomach muscles stiffen.

'Go, Derek,' she ordered softly.

For answer Derek's arms tightened once more.

'I suggest you *do* go.' Blye's voice was even.

'I'm staying here to protect Nicola.'

Sweet of him, but unwise. Almost unconsciously Nicola noted the difference between the two men, the older one tall and broad, with the muscled chest and arms of an athlete; the younger man smaller, frailer, more vulnerable. It was an unfair comparison, but she had made it instinctively.

'I don't need any protection,' she said, and knew it was true. Blye's arrogance was undoubted, but he would not hurt her. She knew she would trust him with her life, if not with her happiness and peace of mind.

'Go, Derek,' Blye said again. His tone was

polite—he would hardly speak otherwise to a paying member of Delayney Tours—but Nicola wondered if the younger man heard the ring of steel.

'I'm staying.'

'Nicola's room is off limits. I must insist that you go.'

If you don't I will throw you out bodily, the cool tone suggested to Nicola's frantic brain.

'Go, Derek,' she said.

Something in both their voices must have got through to him, for his arms loosened. There was defiance in his face, but there was also uncertainty. He must have known that he was no match for Blye.

'Nicola is my girl.' He threw the words into the tension-filled silence.

In the tanned gaunt face there was a thinning of lips, a slight tightening of the jaw. Then Blye said, 'On this tour she is a staff member. As such her quarters are forbidden to you.'

Derek did not seem to know what to say. He left the room with an air of bravado, but Nicola saw that he was humiliated, and knew that Blye had seen it too.

'So,' said Blye, 'Derek *is* your swain?'

Nicola shrugged. From beneath her long eyelashes she darted him a provocative smile. 'I'd say actions speak for themselves, wouldn't you?'

'Don't you have better taste?' Blye's tone was scathing.

'Derek is a very nice person.'

'Nice? By heaven, Nicola, don't ever call *me* nice! I don't think I could stand it. Is your Derek a good lover?'

'Excellent.'

'Does he arouse you?' A hand went to her chin,

forcing her to look at him. Her throat burned where his fingers touched it.

'Yes.' Nicola's temples were pounding.

Now both hands went to her hair, threading through it, cupping her face. 'Do you respond to him?'

The pounding had grown louder—surely he could hear it?—and her heartbeat was frantic. 'Yes,' her voice was unnecessarily loud, 'of course I respond.'

'Strange.'

Blye was so close to her that she could sense every muscle in his body. Swept by an ache that was becoming rapidly familiar, Nicola swayed towards him, then realising what she was doing she made herself stiff.

'For a warm-blooded female,' Blye went on, his tone lazy once more and tinged with insolence, 'you seemed very wooden when Derek was kissing you.'

I can take just so much of this. You know what you're doing to me, and you're enjoying it, damn you!

'It was just a kiss,' she said, surprised that she could sound so cool.

'I haven't kissed you yet, and I can feel you responding.'

She had to divert him. Quickly.

'How was this morning's drive?' she asked.

He laughed. 'That's my Nicola, adept at changing the subject when it gets too hot for her!'

Hot was right. She was burning—with confusion; even more with a wanting for something she could never have.

From somewhere she found the strength to push away his hands. He offered no resistance, and she took a step away from him.

'Well, Blye, how did it go?' she asked again.

'We saw quite a bit.'

'Did anyone miss me?'

'Everybody.'

'Not Gloria,' came the quick retort.

'Gloria more than anyone else.'

'Tell me another one, Blye!'

'It's true.' He grinned. Tiny lights warmed the blue eyes. 'Without you, there was no one for Gloria to tease.'

Nicola's head jerked up. Was Blye on her side after all?

'You've changed your mind about the apology,' she said gladly.

'No.'

'The terms are still the same?'

'Yes.'

'Does it mean so much to you that I should apologise to Gloria?' she asked dully.

Very quietly Blye said, 'Yes, my dear, it does.'

She could not meet his eyes, did not want him to see the pain that racked her. Abruptly she turned and went to stand at the window.

On the hard hot ground beyond the bungalow a few jays squabbled. Nicola's eyes were so blurred with tears that she could not make out the vivid jewel blue of the tiny bodies.

'Why don't you give in?' she heard Blye ask, and realised that he had come up behind her.

Why indeed? At one point—was it only yesterday?—it had seemed very important to stand her ground. She had felt she was fighting for something. Something worth fighting for. But now that Blye had admitted quite how much Gloria meant to him it seemed as if there was nothing to fight for at all.

'What happened to my gutsy lady?' He spoke very softly.

He was so close behind her that she could sense the long hard length of him, the tautness of muscled thighs, the hardness of narrow hips.

'Remember that lady, Nicola?' His arms had folded around her. She could feel the warmth of his body at her back, and the pounding of his heart. She wondered if he could feel her heart beneath his hands.

'Remember, Nicola?'

Her throat was so full that she could not speak. She shook her head.

'I do.' His breath fanned the back of her neck, and she thought she felt his lips in her hair.

After a moment he went on. 'She was so spirited, the Nicola who came into my office for her interview, brave and independent to the point of recklessness. Nothing that would stand in the way of her goals. Remember?'

Yes, she remembered. The Nicola he spoke of was a girl who had been rejected by a man who was now so hazy in her mind that she could barely visualise his features. A girl who had been enthusiastic and eager, her heart set on a new life and determined to succeed at it. A very different girl from the one who stood at the window, so deeply in love with the man behind her that all else paled in importance.

'What happened to that gutsy lady, Nicola? Where is she?'

She opened her mouth to speak, closed it again.

'Is an apology so difficult for her to make that she would let her career crumble because of it?'

Very quietly Nicola said, 'I'll apologise.'

She heard the hiss of his breath, felt it on her hair, then he was turning her in his arms, bringing her around to face hm.

'You mean that?'

'Yes.'

He must think his eloquence had won her over. Let him think it! Rather that, than that he should know the truth—that she realised she had been fighting for a love which could never be hers.

'I'm glad,' he said. 'We'll finish the tour as we started. Apart from us, only Gloria and Derek will know what happened.'

He bent his head. He was going to kiss her. It was the one thing she could not face—not now. She moved out of the circle of his arms.

'My clothes,' she demanded.

'You'll get them.' His voice was odd.

Not quite sure why her blood was racing, she held out a hand. 'Now.'

Ignoring the gesture, he said, 'I'm going to dress you.'

'What!' She stared at him disbelievingly, and wished she could quell her excitement.

'I'm going to dress you,' he said again.

She gave her head a firm shake. 'You're crazy, Blye. After all you've done!'

'Do you think I liked doing it?' he asked roughly.

'You enjoyed every moment of it!'

'This is what I enjoy.' He reached for her and drew her against him. 'What we both enjoy.'

'Get out, Blye!' If only her voice did not sound quite so weak.

'I didn't want to take your clothes, you gave me no choice.' She felt him talk against her hair. 'I want to kiss you.'

I want you to kiss me. Oh, how I want it!

'No, Blye.'

'Yes, love.'

Love. He didn't know the first thing about love. Nicola wished she felt less excited.

'Get out of here!' she muttered.

A tongue licked an earlobe, then he whispered 'No.'

Excitement was making her vulnerable. She should be able to push him away, to put up a fight, to show that she was angry, but her limbs were treacherously weak.

'Please,' she managed.

He looked down at her. 'Please make love to me, is that what you're saying?'

'No!'

'It's what your body is saying.' Mockery in his tone, but tenderness too. 'I prefer to listen to your body.'

And what could she say to that? At least, she thought with satisfaction, if she wanted him, he wanted her too. His body told its own tale, she could feel the heat of it through his safari suit, and the tightening of his muscles. His eyes were dark and intense and filled with a kind of wonder.

'What are you thinking?' she whispered.

'How much I've missed being with you.' He groaned suddenly, and then he was kissing her, deep hungry kisses, demanding response. Nicola did not rationalise. Flooded with a desire that was like nothing she had ever known, she opened her mouth willingly to his, returning kiss for kiss. Her arms went around his neck as she arched her body towards his.

She did not resist as he slid the nightdress from

her shoulders. The touch of his hands on her breasts gave such pleasure that she let out an involuntary moan. His lips followed where his hands had touched, and Nicola thought she would burst with love and longing.

Very gently he put her from him. She looked at him, dazed. 'Blye?' she asked dazedly.

'I shouldn't have started this,' he said raggedly. 'You're so lovely, Nicola, and I want you so much, but I should have had more sense.'

It was hot in the room, yet she felt suddenly chilled. 'What are you trying to say?'

'That we're starting something we can't finish. This isn't the right time, Nicola. Let's wait for the right time, my dearest.'

The endearment meant nothing to her. She hardly heard it. She knew only that she had been rejected—a very bitter rejection in the light of her own too obvious ardour.

The slap across his right cheek stung her hand. 'Just give me my things and then get out!' she shouted at him.

The right time. There would be no right time. She tugged on her clothes with movements made awkward by grief and anger. There would be no time at all. Tomorrow, when the safari ended, she would tell Blye that she was leaving Delayney Tours. The thought of staying on after all that had happened was not to be endured.

The tour ended with more warmth than it had begun. There were hugs and exchanges of addresses between people who had started out as strangers and were now friends. Promises to write and to visit. The Slades issued an open invitation to anyone travelling to New York, and Maria and Anton, smiles wide, managed to say, 'Very nice, very nice,' in an accent that was husky and melodious.

'You were wonderful, Nicola,' said Mrs Barnes, and one after another the others echoed the sentiment. Derek accompanied his own compliment with a kiss. Despite the hollow feeling inside her, Nicola was touched.

Only Gloria kept herself apart—but Gloria had Blye. The brittly beautiful face showed signs of an inexplicable strain, but the hand on his arm was as possessive as ever. Nicola tried not to look at it.

Nicola's smile concealed her own strain. She had told Blye that she was leaving, and he had informed her that that was impossible. Did she not remember the contract she had signed? She was obliged to guide two more tours—anything less would make it unrewarding for Delayney Tours to train staff.

'I won't do it,' Nicola had declared, eyes wide in a face numb with shock.

'You have no option.'

'I could refuse.'

'And be blacklisted by every touring company in the country?'

'You could release me,' she said uncertainly, and knew even before he replied that he would not do it.

There was consolation of a kind in the knowledge that the next tours would be without Blye. The owner of Delayney Tours would not be driving a bus again.

The second tour was pleasant and uneventful.

Game was plentiful and the passengers were a goodhumoured bunch. Not a Gloria among them. Tom, the driver, was a silent young man who was happy to follow all Nicola's suggestions. There were no major problems, no conflict or trauma.

There was also no excitement. Nothing that would live for ever in Nicola's mind.

There were occasions when Nicola had to visit the offices of Delayney Tours. Not once did she see Blye. She never asked about him.

She had rented a room on a weekly basis, not knowing how long she would need it. She had sent out resumés to a number of touring companies. There had been one promising reply, and an interview had been scheduled. The idea did not frighten her. No interview could be like the first one. No interviewer would be Blye.

Derek lived in Nelspruit, and now and then Nicola saw him. They went to two movies together, and afterwards Derek asked if he could come in for coffee.

'It's late,' she smiled up at him the first time.

He made a mock grimace. 'You don't like me.'

'I'm crazy about you,' she teased. 'But it *is* late, Derek.'

'I can take a hint,' he growled. 'Bet you wouldn't turn Blye away.'

The smile left Nicola's face. 'I haven't seen Blye since we got back.'

'Sorry about that,' he said with a gentleness that revealed that he knew how she felt about Blye, that he also knew about Gloria. Leaning forward, he touched her cheek. 'See you soon, Nicola.'

Perhaps she should have let him come inside, Nicola thought, as she watched him drive away. Derek was her only friend in the town. He was an uncomplicated young man, who made no secret of the fact that she was not the only girl he dated. He was fun to be with.

He would have kissed her. Perhaps he would have tried to make love to her. It might not have been a bad thing. The sooner she became accustomed to the attentions of other men, the sooner she would stop brooding about Blye.

Except that there would always be the comparison—an involuntary comparison, perhaps. And there would always be the loving. 'I'm a one-man woman' Nicola realised with despair.

'Bought your ticket for the dance?' asked the receptionist when Nicola arrived at the Delayney Tour offices for details of the third tour.

'I hadn't thought of going.'

'Oh, but you must!' The girl looked at her in surprise. 'It's the event of the year. Besides, the staff are expected to attend.'

'Only staff?' Nicola asked as casually as she could. 'Do the directors come? The ... the president of the company?'

'Not them,' came the cheerful reply. 'Perhaps the disco music puts them off.'

'Does one go alone?'

'No rule about that. Partners are welcome.'

Nicola's chin rose, and into hazel eyes came the light of battle her friend Maggie would have recognised. She would not stay home because of Blye. 'Two tickets, please,' she requested.

'You'll come with me, Derek?' she asked later that evening.

'It means breaking a date, but for you, Nicola'—he chuckled seductively—'it's worth it.'

'You really are a ladies' man!' She could not help laughing. 'Just after eight, then?'

She saw Blye almost immediately. Tall and distinguished, he was a superb-looking man in a sleek dark suit. He was alone.

He saw her in the same moment. There were people on the floor between them, but as their eyes held it was as if they were in the bungalow once more, just two people in a small and empty room. Nicola halted in mid-step, her breath stopped in shock.

'Keep smiling,' advised a low voice as a protective arm went around her shoulders. 'And don't forget for a moment that you're the loveliest girl in the room.'

It came as a revelation to realise that Derek was more than a pleasant young man who liked to flirt and make jokes—he was also kind and unexpectedly sensitive.

'I don't care about Blye,' Nicola said fiercely. 'Please dance with me, Derek.'

The music was lively and they danced together well. A stranger watching the graceful girl in the sky-blue chiffon dress would have said that she was enjoying herself. Nobody would have guessed that her temples were throbbing, that she was aware every moment of a tall tanned man with a rugged face. Nobody but Derek, perhaps. Nicola wondered quite how much he had guessed.

Once Blye danced past them. His partner was a pretty girl with red hair and an adoring expresson. As Blye caught her eye once more, Nicola put her arms around Derek's neck. She thought she saw Blye's jaw tighten a fraction, but the sight did little to lessen her misery. It had been a mistake, after all, to come to the dance. She hated to see another woman in Blye's arms.

So far she had not seen Gloria, but that the woman was here she had no doubt.

Would Blye ask her to dance? she wondered. Time passed, and she understood at last that he would not. Her face muscles ached with the pain of the smile she had forced all night, but the real ache was within her.

Such a short time ago she had been in Blye's arms. Had their lovemaking meant nothing to him? Had she just been one more in a long string of girls? Gloria had warned her, and she had not heeded the warning.

It was getting late. The lights were low and the tempo of the band changed. Slower music now, as if the musicians had understood that couples wanted to be wrapped in each other's arms.

Time to go, Nicola thought. And then she heard someone ask, 'May I cut in?' and her breath jerked in her throat.

'I couldn't come to you until now,' he said as he drew her to him.

'Some kind of protocol?' She threw him a provocative glance. 'Does the most junior member of staff wait in line till the end?'

He laughed softly, the familiar laugh that did such alarming things to her pulse-rate. 'I'd hoped she wouldn't mind waiting for the right music.' His arms closed around her. 'Dim lights and slow music for us, Nicola.'

Memories flooded back. Memories which she had tried so hard to banish from her mind because they brought too much pain. She had never quite succeeded, for though she could discipline herself during the day, she had no control over her dreams at night.

Memories of Blye, standing at the fence and scouring the bush for game, or sitting by the camp-fire and strumming his guitar. Blye holding her, making love to her. Blye in a safari suit that revealed and enhanced the tanned muscularity of a superb body. A very different Blye from the one who held her now, clad in a dark suit of expensive cloth and impeccable cut.

And yet not different at all, Nicola thought, as memory blended with reality. The long hard body so close to hers was as she remembered it; the tautness of strong thighs, the slope of the chest. Against her cheek she felt the beat of his heart, and in her nose was an intoxicating male smell that was like nothing else.

The movements of his legs against hers were tormentingly sensual, and his hands were fire on the bare skin of her back. She could feel his lips in her hair, and she let herself relax against him, cursing herself for a foolishness which she would surely live to regret. They moved slowly, two bodies as one, and it seemed to Nicola as if they were quite alone on the dance-floor. She thought of the first evening of the tour, when she and Blye had sung together by the fire. Then too it was as if the world had belonged to them. Magic had lurked in the darkness around the camp-fire, as well as a fierce kind of joy. So much had happened since that evening. She closed her eyes, as if by so doing she could make that memory the only reality.

'How have you been, Nicola?' she heard him ask.

She tilted her head back to look at him and quelled the longing to touch his face. 'Fine,' she lied. 'And you?'

'I've missed you.'

Not in the way that I've missed you. You could have made an effort to see me, it would have been so simple. Nice words all the same.

'No one to thwart you or give you backchat,' she teased him.

'There's only one Nicola.' He sounded amused. 'Another tour coming up soon, I believe.'

'The third. My last one, Blye.'

If he had meant what he'd said about missing her, now was his chance to tell her not to leave Delayney Tours, not to go back home.

He said instead, 'I hope the tour will be a memorable one.' And then, before she could analyse the strangeness of his tone, he asked, 'Been seeing a lot of Derek?'

'All the time.' He did not react. Had she expected him to? 'How is Gloria?' she asked politely. 'I don't see her here tonight.'

'She didn't come, and I believe she's fine.'

'I'm glad.'

Laughter bubbled in Blye's throat. 'Another lie. You're not glad at all, my Nicola, and you don't want to talk about Gloria. Nor do I.' He drew her close once more, and she closed her eyes, wishing the dance would never end.

One slow song had given way to another when Derek cut in and claimed her once more.

'Did you have to do that?' asked Nicola, when Blye was out of earshot.

'I did it for you.'

'For me?' Hazel eyes were dark and bewildered.

'Blye beckons and you go running,' Derek said grimly.

'You make me sound such a weakling!'

'No, sweetheart, a weakling you're not. But you are a woman in love.'

'Is it so obvious?' she asked on a dry throat.

'To me it is. I kiss you and there's no response at all.' He grinned ruefully. 'I suspect the only man you respond to is Blye.'

'There's not much hope for me if that's the case.' Nicola tried to return the grin and wondered if he saw the glitter of tears in her eyes.

'Perhaps, perhaps not. Make Blye run, Nicola.'

'He may not want to.'

'Then he's not your man. You came here with me, Nicola, you'll leave with me too. Blye will find you if that's what he wants.'

'You're quite a man,' Nicola said unsteadily.

'May I convince you of that?' He pretended to leer down at her.

'Some very lucky girl won't need any convincing. Would you mind if I asked you to take me home now, Derek? I think I need to be alone.'

The days passed and Blye made no effort to contact her. On the day of the tour Nicola made her way to the bus depot with a heavy heart. The driver was a young man called Larry, and the bus was empty. He had instructions to take her to a different depot, he said.

At an inn a little way out of the city they stopped. 'This is the depot?' asked Nicola.

'This is the place. Go inside, miss, tell them you're here.'

'I don't understand,' she said, bewildered.

'I'm taking this bus back to town. You'll be transferring to another one.'

As she made her way across the parking lot Nicola wonderd why the office had notified only

Larry of the change in plans. Hers not to question the ways in which Delayney Tours operated, she supposed. Not that it mattered. This would be her last tour, she might as well take things as they came. Evidently she was early, for there was no bus in the deserted parking lot. There was only one vehicle in sight, grey and expensive-looking. She gave it no more than a cursory glance; her heart was heavy with the knowledge that the tour marked the end of her association with the tour company and that she would not see Blye again.

'Miss Sloane,' said the desk clerk, 'we've been expecting you. This way, please.'

As he led her into a room midway down a long corridor, she looked around her in astonishment. A small living-room, nicely furnished. At one end, by a bay window, was a table set for two, with good cutlery and wine-glasses and a solitary rose in a small glass vase.

The clerk was leaving the room when she called after him, 'There must be some mistake.'

The door closed and she wondered if he had heard her. She was about to follow him when a familiar voice said, 'No mistake.'

For several moments Nicola stood quite rigid. Then, very slowly, she turned. Blye had stood up from a deep armchair which faced out into the garden; she understood why she had not seen him when she'd come into the room.

He came to her and took one of her hands. 'Hello, Nicola.'

She moistened dry lips. 'Hello, Blye.' And then, 'There really is some mistake.'

'No, my dear.'

'I'm off on tour.'

'So you are. After breakfast.'

Feeling giddy, she allowed herself to be coaxed into a chair. Her eyes fell on a bottle reposing in a bucket of ice. 'Wine, Blye? For breakfast?'

'Champagne, actually. Goes well with eggs Benedict.'

'Champagne for breakfast? I don't believe it!'

'Only one glass. I wouldn't risk befuddling you with more at this time of the morning.' He was laughing, and as she looked up and met his eyes she knew to what he referred.

Bemused, she watched as he uncorked the bottle. Then she said, 'Blye, what's going on?'

'First a toast. Then we'll talk.'

'A toast to what?'

'To our tour.'

She stared at him. 'You're going to drive again?'

'If you'll let me.'

A quiver shot through her at the odd turn of phrase. 'There was no bus in the parking lot. Just one car, in fact.' A thought struck her. 'Your car, Blye?'

'Yes.'

'Where's the bus?'

'Don't you want to know about the tour?'

'Blye, the bus ... the passengers. . . .' she began.

'Paris, Rome, and then Capri,' he said. 'Wait till you look out to sea from Anacapri, Nicola.'

She was dreaming, she knew it. She was also trembling. 'Delayney Tours don't go to Capri.'

'Honeymoons do.'

The trembling had increased quite alarmingly as she said, 'Don't tease me, Blye.'

'I'm not teasing, my darling.' He reached

across the table for her hand, turned it palm upwards and kissed it. And all the time he was looking at her, and in his eyes she saw an expression she had never seen there before: uncertainty. Blye Peterson, Beldon Delayney, was uncertain of himself!

'I love you so much. Will you marry me, Nicola?'

Hazel eyes, wide and luminous, looked back at him through a haze of joy. 'I'm dreaming! There's Gloria.'

'There's no Gloria. There never has been.'

'But she said. . . . And Mrs Barnes read it in the papers.'

'Let me tell you about Gloria. Briefly.' Blye's voice was hard. 'She wanted a divorce and had no definite grounds for one. I was content to play along with her. We were seen together, photographed together. The Delayney name made me a notorious co-respondent. Perhaps I was a fool, but her husband was an utter swine, and I had no attachments. The women I knew were only after quick sex or money. There was no one I cared for.'

He paused, and the blue eyes were lit with a gleam that sent the adrenalin pumping fast through Nicola's nerve-stream. 'Little did I guess that things could change!'

'Did they change?' she asked demurely.

'In a moment I'll take great pleasure in telling you quite how much.' His grin was wicked. 'Let's get Gloria over first. She couldn't accept the façade for what it was, and she began to follow me. She discovered that I was going to drive the tour and made a last-minute reservation. I'm afraid she became a pest.'

'Not such a pest,' Nicola said spiritedly, 'that you didn't enjoy kissing her.'

'Ah! You had to catch us in the trees that day. I'd told her there could be nothing between us, and she was trying to persuade me otherwise.' He still had her hand and now he began to stroke it. 'I'm thirty-four and I'm not a saint. But Gloria was never my mistress.'

'Then why was it so important that I apologise to her?'

'I wanted her to know that the woman I love has class. That she doesn't kick others when she doesn't get her way—oh yes, I saw that kick in the bus—that she doesn't throw tantrums.'

'That she's never rude.' Nicola's eyes danced with mischief. 'Especially when the customer is wrong.'

'Exactly.'

Hazel eyes turned serious. 'What value was there in a forced apology?'

'Gloria didn't know it was forced. Along with the rest of the group she was told you were ill.'

'Blye, you're a devil!'

'I know, my darling, but I do adore you. Will you marry me, Nicola?'

She looked at the tanned face with its gaunt cheeks and strongly-defined angles, and wondered if she had ever been quite as happy as she was at this moment.

'There's something else I must know,' she said.

'Do you know that you're torturing me?'

She laughed, and the sound was high and joyous. 'Derek said I should let you do some running.'

'Wretched Derek! There were times when I came near to throttling him.'

'He wouldn't have deserved it; he's the kindest man I know. There was never anything between us, Blye. The night of the dance he tried to help me.'

'You'll want to name our first-born after him, I suppose.'

She could feel her heart pounding. 'Very likely. Blye, I have to know—when John was ill and you took his place, did you know I'd be guiding the tour?'

For answer Blye rose from his chair and walked around the table. He drew Nicola to her feet and then his hands cupped her shoulders. 'John wasn't ill, my darling Nicola. He was given paid leave.'

Joy was a wild thing in her throat. 'By you?'

'I fell in love with you at the interview. I had to get to know you, and what better way than by spending some time in your company? Now, Nicola, could you bear to answer my question—*will* you marry me?'

'Oh yes, my darling, yes!'

She was in his arms then, and he was kissing her, and she was responding kiss for kiss. The door opened, and the waiter brought in a tray. As he put it down quietly he thought what a good thing it was that eggs Benedict would keep.

THE SCULPTURE OF ANCIENT GREECE

A man's physical attractiveness is highly praised indeed, if his looks are compared favorably to that of a Greek statue—which is exactly what Nicola does when she looks at Blye. For the sculptors of ancient Greece carved beautiful statues of gods, goddesses and mortals, usually athletes, which, until the art of the European Renaissance more than fifteen centuries later, were unequaled in realism, proportion and beauty.

Early Greek sculptures were stiff and squarish, but around the fourth century B.C. the best artists of Athens began to faithfully reproduce movement in marble, limestone or wood, casting the latter in bronze, gold or silver. A statue of a young man standing on one leg, the other leg stepping forward, might be carved. Or an athlete portrayed at a moment of concentration, about to spring into a run. Or a bronze Zeus carved with one arm raised, poised to hurl lightning bolts across the sky.

Most particularly, Greek sculptors loved beauty. Polyclitus, one of the most famous artists, carved the *Doryphorus*, or spear carrier. This statue was said to have a perfectly proportioned body and therefore, the artist claimed, perfect beauty.

Greek statues could be small, life-size or enormous. The sculptor Phidias cast a gigantic bronze statue of the goddess Athena, which stood on the Acropolis high above Athens and was seen by travelers on ships approaching from afar.

Tragically, the ravages of time have taken their toll on these beautiful works of art. While the Romans made hundreds of copies, only a few dozen of the original Greek statues survive. Such famous ones as *Winged Victory, Venus de Milo, Discus Thrower* and *Belvedere Apollo* can be seen in the world's great museums.

ROBERTA LEIGH

Collector's Edition

A specially designed collection of six exciting love stories by one of the world's favorite romance writers—Roberta Leigh, author of more than 60 bestselling novels!

1 **Love in Store**   4 **The Savage Aristocrat**
2 **Night of Love**   5 **The Facts of Love**
3 **Flower of the Desert**   6 **Too Young to Love**

Available now wherever paperback books are sold, or available through Harlequin Reader Service. Simply complete and mail the coupon below.

Harlequin Reader Service

In the U.S.
P.O. Box 52040
Phoenix, AZ 85072-9988

In Canada
649 Ontario Street
Stratford, Ontario N5A 6W2

Please send me the following editions of the Harlequin Roberta Leigh Collector's Editions. I am enclosing my check or money order for $1.95 for each copy ordered, plus 75¢ to cover postage and handling.

☐ 1   ☐ 2   ☐ 3   ☐ 4   ☐ 5   ☐ 6

Number of books checked_____ @ $1.95 each = $_____
N.Y. state and Ariz. residents add appropriate sales tax $_____
Postage and handling $_____.75_____
                     TOTAL $_____

I enclose_____
(Please send check or money order. We cannot be responsible for cash sent through the mail.) Price subject to change without notice.

NAME_____
                  (Please Print)
ADDRESS_____ APT. NO._____
CITY_____
STATE/PROV._____ ZIP/POSTAL CODE_____

Offer expires February 29, 1984   30856000000

RL-N